LO

12/09

The
Trouble
with
MARK HOPPER

The
Trouble
with
MARK HOPPER

ELISSA BRENT WEISSMAN

3 1336 08381 9897

DUTTON CHILDREN'S BOOKS

DUTTON CHILDREN'S BOOKS
A division of Penguin Young Readers Group

Published by the Penguin Group • Penguin Group (USA) Inc., 375 Hudson Street,
New York, New York 10014, U.S.A. • Penguin Group (Canada), 90 Eglinton Avenue
East, Suite 700, Toronto, Ontario M4P 2Y3, Canada (a division of Pearson Penguin
Canada Inc.) • Penguin Books Ltd, 80 Strand, London WC2R 0RL, England
• Penguin Ireland, 25 St Stephen's Green, Dublin 2, Ireland (a division of Penguin
Books Ltd) • Penguin Group (Australia), 250 Camberwell Road, Camberwell,
Victoria 3124, Australia (a division of Pearson Australia Group Pty Ltd) • Penguin
Books India Pvt Ltd, 11 Community Centre, Panchsheel Park, New Delhi - 110 017,
India • Penguin Group (NZ), 67 Apollo Drive, Rosedale, North Shore 0632,
New Zealand (a division of Pearson New Zealand Ltd.) • Penguin Books (South
Africa) (Pty) Ltd, 24 Sturdee Avenue, Rosebank, Johannesburg 2196, South Africa •
Penguin Books Ltd, Registered Offices: 80 Strand, London WC2R 0RL, England

CIP Data is available.

Published in the United States by Dutton Children's Books,
a division of Penguin Young Readers Group
345 Hudson Street, New York, New York 10014
www.penguin.com/youngreaders

Designed by Elizabeth Frances

Printed in USA   First Edition

ISBN 978-0-525-42067-5   10 9 8 7 6 5 4 3 2 1

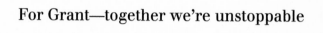

For Grant—together we're unstoppable

Contents

The
Trouble
with
MARK HOPPER

Chapter

1

The Hoppers

Mark Geoffrey Hopper had brown hair that he wore gelled in a side part, blue eyes, and a splattering of freckles across his face that made him look like he'd fallen asleep on a freshly laid gravel driveway. He usually wore khaki pants, a tucked-in shirt, and a look that said he would not only get further than you in this afternoon's geography bee, but he would look cuter doing it, too.

Mark Geoffrey Hopper had brown hair that he wore parted to the side, though without gel, blue eyes, and a spread of freckles across his face that looked like they'd been splattered on with a paintbrush. He usually wore khaki pants, a tucked-in shirt, and a look that said he was impressed with everything around him, though he wasn't quite sure how he got there.

Mark Geoffrey Hopper did not really look like Mark Geoffrey

Hopper, but if you were describing him to the principal because he'd called you a dim-witted doofus, or to a friend because you had a crush on him, you would describe him the same way. That was the trouble with Mark Hopper and Mark Hopper. Well, that and the fact that they had the same name.

Mark Hopper had lived in Greenburgh, Maryland, and had argued with most of its residents, for all eleven years of his life. The teachers at Ivy Road Middle School were tired just thinking that they might have Mark Hopper in their class when he started at the school next year, as they had just—finally!—gotten rid of Mark's older sister Beth, whose mouth was just as big and permanently sneered as her younger brother's. Beth didn't think school could teach her anything useful, and she made a point, daily, of asking each of her teachers how each lesson could possibly help her in real life. She was never absent, though—not once—since school was a good place to pull pranks. She'd pull them indiscriminately, on both teachers and students, which made her about as popular with her classmates as she was with the faculty. But that didn't stop her. On her last day of eighth grade, Beth placed gum on every seat in every classroom on her schedule. She then prided herself on having everyone stand in her honor all day. Mark prided himself on everything.

The other Mark Hopper and his mother and sister moved into Greenburgh the summer before Mark was to start Ivy Road Middle School. And this Mark's older sister Beth was just as quiet and pleasant as her little brother. Unlike Beth Hopper, Beth Hopper wasn't going to the local high school in Greenburgh, but to the Lefko School for Science, where she was getting a scholarship to do one of her favorite things: research earthworms.

When she found out that she was accepted to the Lefko School and that she had gotten a scholarship, she kissed her favorite earthworm, Inty (so named for his internal circulatory system—all of her earthworms were named for their physiological features), right in front of Mark and some of his friends. After a few weeks of being called "Worm Lover" by everyone except his best friend, Sammy, Mark was kind of looking forward to moving to Greenburgh and starting at a new school.

Moving to Greenburgh also meant that Mark would get to spend lots of time with his grandpa, Murray. Mrs. Hopper found a nice big house for all of them: Mark, Beth, Grandpa Murray, herself, and her husband, who was only going to be living there on occasional weekends and holidays until he could find a job closer to Greenburgh and sell their old house in Massachusetts. Mark and Beth missed their father and couldn't wait for him to move in with them permanently, but they loved living with Grandpa Murray. He was absentminded when it came to things like picking up after himself—he left half-eaten apples on the kitchen table, half-read newspapers on the living room couch, his underwear on the bathroom floor after half a day—which their mom said had always been the case, but he never failed in coming up with ways to make everyday tasks fun, such as inventing themes for their dinners. Mark and Beth's favorite was the caveman dinner, which involved eating all of the food with their hands, using a rock or leaf for a napkin, and communicating only in grunts. In response, Mrs. Hopper suggested a royalty theme that required being very clean and polite and proper, but that idea was democratically voted down, three to one.

Mark and Beth Hopper would surely have enjoyed the

caveman dinner, too—though they probably would have been more rowdy cavemen—if they knew Grandpa Murray and the Hoppers, which they didn't; not yet. And since the Hoppers had just moved in, they didn't yet know the Hoppers, either. But the Hoppers wanted to become a part of the community in their new town; they didn't realize that most people in Greenburgh had the same reaction to the name Hopper as they did to the term *routine dental work*. That was the trouble with the Hoppers and the Hoppers. Well, that and the fact that they had the same name.

Chapter 2

Mark Hopper

Mark Hopper was smart. And he knew it. But he wasn't smart enough to know that nobody wanted to be reminded all the time of how smart he was and how he knew it. That was the main trouble with Mark Hopper.

The main trouble for people who knew Mark Hopper was that disagreeing with him was more hassle than it was worth. So he usually got his way. Which only made disagreeing with him more trouble.

For example: Mark got a perfect score on every spelling test in fifth grade, but on one test toward the end of the year he got a ninety-five because he spelled *cooperate* like *co-operate*. That was the British spelling, and he knew it, so he argued with his teacher, but she would not raise his score to a hundred; she argued that they lived in America. In fact, the only reason Mark spelled *cooperate* as *co-operate* was that he knew it was the British spelling, and he wanted to argue with his teacher. And his teacher, and the rest of the class, suspected it. So when Miss Kelly wouldn't cooperate (or co-operate), he made an appointment with the principal of Farrow Park Elementary School, Mr. Graham.

"I have gotten a perfect score on every spelling test this year," Mark said, pacing Mr. Graham's office in his khaki pants and tucked-in shirt and side-parted, gelled hair. "I do not think it is fair to penalize me for using the British spelling of the word *cooperate.* It is a perfectly good way to spell the word; it's just different. We did a whole unit this year about different cultures and how we have to be accepting of different people. In fact," Mark added, "I got one hundred percent on my diorama about Sweden."

This was not the first time Principal Graham had watched Mark pace and listened to him argue. It wasn't even the first time he had seen Mark that *week,* for Mark had made an appointment to tell him that Frank Stucco had pushed J. T. Morris into a tree at recess on Monday. That time, Mr. Graham had told Mark to mind his own business, unless it was a very serious matter. This time, he thanked Mark for his mature argument, but told him that since he was in school in America, he was learning to spell things in American English. "If you spelled the word *cooperate* in Swedish, you would lose points, too," Principal Graham said.

Mark sneered.

"Besides," the principal went on, "it is not so bad to not get a hundred on every single test."

Mark narrowed his freckled forehead. "We'll see what your boss says about that."

He wrote a letter to the superintendent:

Dear Superintendent Griswold,

My name is Mark Hopper and I am in fifth grade at Farrow Park Elementary School. I am in Miss Kelly's class. I have gotten a score of 100 percent on every spelling test this year. But then on our last spelling test, I got a 95 because I used the correct British spelling of co-operate. Miss Kelly said it would have to be spelled cooperate. Principal Graham agreed for some dumb reason. This is not fair. I am the smartest person in Miss Kelly's class and probably in the whole fifth grade at Farrow Park Elementary School. Actually I am probably the smartest person in the whole fifth grade in all of Greenburgh. Why should the smartest fifth grader in all of Greenburgh (and maybe in all of Maryland but probably not the whole country, but who knows) lose points on a spelling test because my teacher does not accept things that are different? What can you do about this? It is an outrage.

Your friend,
Mark Geoffrey Hopper

When the superintendent did not respond to the letter in three days, Mark called his office and left a message with his secretary. And when the superintendent did not return the call within twenty-four hours, Mark rode his bicycle to his office and sat in the waiting room until he saw him.

"I used the right British spelling," Mark explained, his arms crossed and his voice hostile.

The superintendent scratched his head. "You don't sound British," he said.

"I'm not British," said Mark impatiently. "But I am accepting of other cultures. I got one hundred percent on my diorama about Sweden."

"Are you Swedish?" asked the superintendent, who was more confused than ever.

"What?" said Mark, who thought the superintendent was missing the point.

Mr. Griswold stroked his gray beard. "Okay, I will make sure you get back those five points on your spelling test. But from now on you have to use the American spellings of words. And you have to cooperate with your teacher."

"Can you put that in writing?" Mark asked.

At school the next morning, Mark marched up to Miss Kelly's desk and smugly handed her his letter from the superintendent. ("Dear Ms. Kelly, Please give your Swedish student his five points back.") Miss Kelly gave him the five points and a weary look.

When Mark got a blue ribbon for spelling, he pinned it to his shirt and wore it all day. The other students laughed, and Frank Stucco pushed him into a tree after school, but Mark just stuck his freckled nose in the air and told them they were jealous.

"Hey, Mark," shouted J. T. Morris. "How do you spell *spitwad*?"

"Look it up, fartbrain," Mark shot back.

Even Jasmina Horace, his only friend—who was probably his friend only because they lived across the street from each other and had been playing together since they were infants—told him to take off the ribbon. "You look stupid," she said.

"No," said Mark with a laugh. "Getting a blue ribbon for spelling makes you *smart*. Duh."

"But wearing it makes you look stupid."

"How could an award for being smart make you look stupid?"

Jasmina, who knew it wasn't worth arguing with Mark, walked away.

"Why are you even friends with him?" Mark heard Kylie ask Jasmina. He then heard Jasmina give the answer she always gave to that question: "I have no idea." Mark stuck out his chin, and his chest with the blue ribbon, and walked home alone.

Chapter 38

Mark Hopper

Mark's bright blue eyes opened with a jolt. He breathed in the smell of grease and ran down the hall, sliding in his slippers on the wood floors into the kitchen. Sure enough, Grandpa Murray was making breakfast, and that meant it'd be an array of deliciously unhealthy food that Mark's mother would hardly ever make, especially all at once. Mark put his chin on the countertop and stared wide-eyed at the spread of sausage, bacon, eggs, and chocolate-chip pancakes frying on the stove. Grandpa Murray, wearing an apron that said PAY THE COOK, hit Mark on the bottom with a spatula. "Don't drool on the food," he said.

"Why not?" said Mark with a big grin. "Maybe it'll taste better than syrup."

"That's disgusting," said Beth. She rubbed her eyes in front of the stove. "Good morning, Grandpa. Thanks for making breakfast."

"I think the pancakes are ready to be flipped. Watch this, kids." Grandpa Murray stuck his spatula under one of the pancakes on the skillet and flicked his wrist. The pancake did a somersault in the air and landed halfway on top of another pancake. "Whoops. Close, though." He used the spatula to separate the pancakes. Then he flipped the second one with extra gusto. It did a three-sixty and landed back on the side that had already been cooked.

Mark and Beth cheered. "Can I try?" Mark asked.

"You get one shot," Grandpa Murray said. "If you can do better than me, I will eat this apron and leave all the food for you and your sister and your mom."

Mark took the spatula and stuck it underneath a small pancake. He flicked his wrist. The pancake flipped up and landed on the countertop, raw side down. Mark raised his eyebrows and stretched his mouth into a sort-of grin. "How was that?"

"C-plus," said Grandpa Murray.

Mark shrugged. That was about the grade he was used to getting.

Mrs. Hopper walked in and eyed the pancake mix dripping down the counter. She said "good morning," but her tone of voice suggested she did not think the morning was particularly good so far.

"Let me try," said Beth. She took the spatula and slid it under a pancake. She scrunched her forehead and her eyes darted back and forth. Then she flicked her wrist, and the pancake flipped gracefully into the air and landed right back in its original spot, raw side down. Beth smiled.

"How did you do that?" Mark asked in amazement.

"Physics," she said with a shrug.

"Speaking of which," Mrs. Hopper said. "You got something from school, Beth."

Beth took the envelope from her mother and opened it up. It was her class schedule. "Cool!" Beth said. "I have three hours in the lab every single day. I can't *wait* for school."

"Cool," said Grandpa Murray. He looked at Mark and rotated his finger around the side of his head. Mark laughed.

Mrs. Hopper clapped her hand over her mouth. "I never registered Mark for school," she said.

"Ah," said Grandpa Murray. "You mentioned that a few weeks ago, didn't you?"

"Does that mean I can't go?" Mark asked hopefully.

"No, it just means I have to call and do it right now."

"Good try," said Grandpa Murray. "Breakfast's up!"

Mrs. Hopper looked up the number for Ivy Road Middle School and dialed.

"Ivy Road Middle School, Ethel speaking," came the voice from the other end. Ethel had been working in the main office of Ivy Road since the school had opened.

"Hello, Ethel," said Mrs. Hopper. "My name is Leslie Hopper, and I'd like to register my son for school."

Ethel, who did not know how to use the computer and refused to learn, took out a piece of paper. "What is your son's name?" she asked.

"Mark Hopper."

"Mark . . . Hopper," Ethel said as she wrote it on the top of the sheet in careful cursive.

"Mark Hopper?" said Mindy, the young office worker sitting next to Ethel. "School hasn't even started and a Hopper's already causing trouble?"

"Excuse me?" said Ethel.

"Excuse me?" said Leslie.

"One moment, dear," said Ethel. She turned to Mindy and asked if Mark Hopper was already enrolled for September.

Mindy snorted. "If he isn't, then all of the teachers have been complaining for nothing." She pulled up Mark Hopper's file on the computer and turned the screen toward Ethel.

"Hello?" said Leslie.

"Hello," said Ethel. "Mrs. Hopper, your son is already enrolled."

"Really?" Leslie turned to her family, who were happily munching on breakfast. "They think Mark's already registered," she said.

Ethel tapped the computer monitor. "I don't know what to do with this box," she said to Mindy.

"Excuse me?" said Leslie.

Mindy took the phone from Ethel. "Hi, Mrs. Hopper," she said. "Mark Geoffrey Hopper, sixth grade?"

"Yes. That's correct."

"Yep, he's already in our computer system. He's all set."

"That's strange," Leslie said. "I know my husband wouldn't have called." She turned to Grandpa Murray. "Did you register Mark for school?"

Grandpa Murray shook his head. Leslie asked if he was

sure. Grandpa Murray chewed thoughtfully on a piece of bacon. "Maybe I did," he said.

Mark laughed.

"Actually, yes, I suppose I did," Grandpa Murray said. "I forgot."

Mindy popped her gum. "Well, I know a lot of teachers are looking forward to having Mark, because of Beth." She looked at her fellow office staff and mouthed, "Yeah, right." A few of them rolled their eyes or shook their heads.

Mrs. Hopper was so surprised she nearly dropped the phone. She was used to people in their old town looking forward to having Mark because of Beth, but she had no idea how anyone in Greenburgh could know anything about Beth. Unless Grandpa Murray had accidentally registered Beth, too. That was something he might do. "Beth isn't registered, is she?" she asked. Everyone at the table gave her a cockeyed look.

"I hope not," said Mindy. "Beth should be starting high school this year."

"Of course," said Leslie. "Just checking."

"Anything else we can help you with, Mrs. Hopper?" asked Ethel, who was back on the line.

"Well, can you just check and make sure he is registered for art?" she said. "I know Mark wants to take art." Mark gave her a thumbs-up.

Ethel consulted Mindy's computer screen. "No, we have him down for band."

Mark's mother laughed. She shook her head at Grandpa Murray. "Can you please change that to art? Mark is definitely not a musician."

"That's for sure," said Beth in a low voice.

Mark stuck out his tongue at her. "Everyone is squeaky when they start learning to play the violin."

Beth shuddered. "Not *that* squeaky."

At Ivy Road, Ethel held a pen poised over a sheet of paper. "Are you absolutely sure he wants art?" she asked. "We can't keep changing it back and forth, you know. Art and band do not meet the same period, so changing that one class means changing the whole schedule. I have to write it down, and then someone needs to enter it into the computer system. That's a lot of work over here, especially with class schedules being mailed the end of the week."

Mrs. Hopper replied, "Yes. Mark is right here and he says he definitely wants art. I'm sorry to cause trouble."

"No trouble," said Ethel politely.

Mindy raised her eyebrows at Ethel. "You mean nothing but trouble. We're talking about the Hoppers here."

"Excuse me?" said Mrs. Hopper.

"Nothing," said Ethel. "Is that all?"

Mrs. Hopper said yes and thanked her before hanging up. Then she turned to Grandpa Murray, who was busy rolling a pancake around a piece of sausage. "Into your blanket, little piggy," he cooed.

"You registered Mark for band," said Mrs. Hopper.

"No," said Grandpa Murray. "I am sure that I registered him for art."

Mrs. Hopper laughed and crossed her arms. "You didn't even remember that you registered him at all!"

"Yes, and I *distinctly* don't remember registering him for band. The fools."

Mark patted Grandpa Murray on the back. "I love you, Grandpa," he said.

His mother shook her head and put some scrambled eggs on her plate.

"It's a good thing you called," Grandpa Murray said. "Some people are just incompetent."

Mark's Schedule

"CAR!" shouted Lou.

Everyone moved to the sides of the street. Mark held his arm in front of six-year-old Timmy Horace. Once the car passed and Lou shouted "SAFE," Mark looked both ways and gave the okay for play to continue. He held Timmy's hand as they walked back into the street. "That's how smart people like me enter the street," he told Timmy. "Always, always look both ways."

Timmy said, "I know, I know," and wriggled his hand away.

Mark resumed his spot on the sewer cap that was a base. Jasmina, who was a better pitcher by anyone's judgment except Mark's, took her place on the Hoppers' garbage-can lid, which was the other base. The five younger kids from the street assumed positions with one foot touching the sewer—they were safe as long as the tip of their sneaker still touched. Lou enjoyed shouting more than running, so he kept his post on the Horaces' stoop to look out for cars.

Jasmina checked her runners and wound up. She threw the ball to Mark and the runners on his base sprinted toward the garbage lid. Mark caught it and threw it back to Jasmina immediately. The runners who had just touched her base squealed and turned around before she could touch them with the ball. Those who hadn't made it all the way across hesitated in the middle. Would she throw it quickly back to Mark? Would she hold it for a few seconds? The object was not to get tagged, and not to get stuck with your foot touching a base while that thrower held the ball. Jasmina fake-threw to Mark, and Timmy, falling for it, sprinted. Jasmina moved to tag him but let Timmy duck out of the way.

"Oh, man!" she said as Timmy dodged her mitt. "Too fast." She threw the ball back to Mark, and Timmy, safe on the garbage lid, jumped up and down.

When Mark caught the ball he crossed his arms. "What was that, Jasmina?" he said angrily. "Timmy was *right there*."

Jasmina raised her eyebrows and tightened her mouth. "He was, but he was just too fast, Mark."

"You cheated," said Mark.

"No. I. Didn't," Jasmina said deliberately, her eyes glaring into Mark's.

The other kids looked around at one another anxiously.

"So you don't think letting someone get away on purpose is cheating? Last time I checked it was."

Timmy looked at his older sister. "Did you let me get away?"

"Are you kidding?" Jasmina said. "I tried to tag you; you saw it. You were just too quick and nimble."

"I bet you don't even know what *nimble* means," Mark said.

Now Jasmina crossed her arms. "How could I have just used it if I don't know what it means?"

"What's *nimble*?" asked Timmy.

"Look it up," said Mark.

"Come on, Mark," said Jasmina. "Let's just get back to the game."

"What's the point in playing if you're just going to let your little brother win? That's not fair to everybody else."

The others looked at one another and started mumbling about Mark being right.

"CAR!" shouted Lou.

Mark moved to the sidewalk in front of his house. The other kids followed him. Timmy started toward that side, but Jasmina grabbed his hand and pulled him toward the opposite side of the street, to their house. "I think it's lunchtime," she said to Timmy. "Go put my mitt inside?"

"SAFE!" shouted Lou.

Mark and the others moved back to position. Jasmina walked up to Mark's sewer. "Something is seriously wrong with you," she said. "He's six years old. And this isn't the Olympics, for pete's sake."

"Exactly. I don't know why you'd bother cheating for just a friendly game in the street. It just ruins it for everyone else."

Jasmina knew Mark wasn't worth losing her temper over. But she was still fuming. "You are the biggest idiot on the planet," she said. "No, in the whole solar system!"

Mark laughed. "If I'm the biggest idiot in the solar system, how come I'm in all honors classes next year? And how come I got a hundred on every single spelling test this year?"

Jasmina shook her head, swishing her hundreds of tiny black braids. "I'm going inside."

"Okay. Come back when you're ready to play fairly," he said.

Jasmina stomped into her house and slammed the door. Mark saw Timmy's face disappear from the front window. "Don't cheat," Mark said to the others. "Or people won't want to be your friend."

"Hey, smart guy!" Jasmina shouted from her window.

Mark looked at the others. "See, she's lonely already. What, Jasmina?"

"We got our schedules in the mail!"

Mark put the ball in someone's hand and sprinted toward his house. Even though he didn't have many friends to compare schedules with, he was excited to see who his teachers were and find out the scoop on them from Beth. And of course he wanted to make sure that it was all correct and that he was in all honors classes. He had a brief flash of himself opening his schedule and finding a letter saying that since he was so smart they were going to put him straight into the seventh grade. He knew that that probably wouldn't happen, but imagine how jealous everyone would be if it did!

Sure enough, in his mailbox was a big envelope from Ivy Road Middle School addressed to "the parent or guardian of Mark Geoffrey Hopper." He tore it open and set aside various pieces of paper—a welcome letter from the principal, a list of important dates, information about buses—until he found his class schedule. First period, social studies 6H with Rocco. He scanned down. 6H, 6H, 6 . . . everything seemed to be sixth-grade classes. But maybe once they all got to see how smart he was, they would move him up. It seemed like a decent schedule—social studies and science and math in the morning; English, computers, gym, and art in the afternoon. Wait. "ART?!" Mark screamed.

Beth came down from her room holding her ears. "What are you yelling about?" she whined.

"They put me in *art*," he said, pronouncing "art" as though it were a class on cleaning up after elephants.

Beth pointed at Mark and laughed. "I didn't realize I had an art-fart for a brother."

"I didn't sign up for it," Mark said. "The stupid people in the office obviously screwed up."

Beth agreed that the people in the office at Ivy Road were stupid. "The worst is Ethel," she said. "She's old and vile. I'm so glad I'm out of that stupid school."

Mark was already dialing the number for Ivy Road. "The line is busy," he said, stamping his foot. "They must have messed up a lot of schedules to have so many people calling."

Beth laughed and laughed. "I'm surprised Ethel knows how to use a telephone," she said through her laughter.

Mark took his schedule, ran outside, and mounted his bicycle. He paused for a moment, then ran back in and grabbed his blue ribbon for spelling and his bassoon practice book, which had a "Good Job!" sticker on every exercise through page sixty-eight. Ribbon pinned on his shirt, schedule in his pocket, and bassoon book tucked under his helmet, he flicked his bike into speed ten and pedaled vigorously to Ivy Road.

Mark's Schedule

Grandpa Murray was teaching Mark and Beth to play blackjack. "Hit me," said Mark.

That's when it hit Beth. "Shouldn't you have gotten your class schedule by now, Mark?" she said.

Mark thought. After she called and found out that he was already registered, his mom had said that they would be mailing the schedules the end of the week. And Grandpa Murray had suddenly remembered that they had told him that when he had registered Mark as well. Mark shrugged. "I guess that means I can't go. Hit me." He didn't see why Beth loved school so much. But he didn't really mind going, despite his jokes. It was just what he did five days a week. Though maybe if he did as well as Beth always did, he would like it more. He knew that no one expected him to be a genius like Beth, but he sometimes wished he was. "Oh, boo," Mark said. "I'm over."

"Why don't you call Ivy Road?" Beth suggested. "See what happened to your schedule. You don't want to show up the first day and not know what to do. Hit me." Grandpa Murray gave her another card, and Beth said, "I'll stay."

"I show up lots of places and don't know what to do," said Grandpa Murray. "You meet nice people that way. I'm going to hit again."

Mark laughed. "Well, I don't know if the people in the office will be the nicest on the first day. They'll probably be really busy. I'll tell Mom to call when she gets home."

"Come on," Beth said. "You're old enough to call yourself."

Mark shrugged his skinny shoulders. He didn't like calling adults on the phone; he never knew what to say. He didn't even really like talking to adults in person. They always asked the same pointless questions, like what grade was he in and what was his favorite subject. He was talkative and funny around people his own age, and around Beth and his parents and his grandpa, but the moment he had to talk to an adult—even a teacher—it was like he'd forget how to form words. That was the main trouble with Mark Hopper. His mom was always suggesting ways to help him be less shy. And so was Beth, even though she always got quiet around adults, too, unless she was talking about earthworms. Last Thanksgiving, when they had gone all the way to Oregon to spend the holiday with a bunch of their dad's cousins they didn't know, Mark and Beth stood next to each other quietly, politely answering the cousins' questions until they could go into another room and play cards.

"What have you got?" Grandpa Murray asked Beth. She revealed a total of twenty. Grandpa Murray threw his cards in the air. "You win again," he said. "I'm going to get this girl a fake ID and take her to Vegas."

Beth blushed and muttered something about it following mathematical rules even though the odds were less than half. "Call the school, Mark," Beth said, changing the subject.

Mark sighed. He would have to practice being more outgoing if he was going to make a good impression at Ivy Road. And his parents would be proud that he took care of something like this by himself. His mom would be especially proud, since she had a lot to do with getting the house in order and starting her job at the bank and didn't really have time to worry about calling Mark's school. He practiced what he should say a few times in his head. Then he got up and dialed the number for Ivy Road School that his mother had written on the whiteboard by the phone. He pressed the numbers at lightning speed; otherwise he knew he would chicken out mid-dial. "Hello," he said in his best grown-up voice. "My name is Mark Hopper and I am going to be in sixth grade this year, but I haven't gotten my class schedule yet, and I was just wondering if you mailed them out already."

"I believe we did mail them out, hon," said the woman on the other end. "But it's my first day here, so let me make sure."

"Okay, thank you." Mark blushed at being called "hon."

"Yes, we mailed them out over a week ago. You should have gotten it by now, hon. What did you say your name was?"

"Mark Hopper. We just moved, so—"

"Oh, you moved? Well, that must be the problem, because I'm sure we mailed them all. Give me your address and I'll change it in the computer."

What was their new address? "Um . . ." How embarrassing to not know his own address! He had just written it in an e-mail to his friend Sammy, who promised to mail him some baseball cards. "Seven forty-three Crown Road."

"All right, hon. I changed it and I'll mail it out right now. Should arrive tomorrow."

It did arrive the next day, and Mark could not believe what was on it. After all of the trouble his mother had gone through, they had him in band instead of art. But even more surprising was that he was in all honors classes. Every one of them, down the line—6H, 6H, 6H—except for lunch, which Mark figured probably wasn't grouped by ability. Too bad, he thought, since he was good at eating and talking and finishing up the homework that was due after lunch.

"Good job, kiddo!" said Grandpa Murray, who was looking over his shoulder. "Those *H*s mean you'll be with all the nerds, right?"

Beth crossed her arms. "People in honors classes aren't nerds, Grandpa."

Mark stared at his schedule with his eyes as round as full moons. After he took the fifth-grade standardized tests, his teacher told him and his parents that he would not make it into any advanced classes in sixth grade, but if he worked hard he could get moved up. "Maybe my old school sent over your grades instead of mine," he said to Beth.

"Maybe they just have different standards in Maryland," Beth said gently. "But good job, Mark."

A smile began to play on Mark's lips. Pretty soon it was as wide as his eyes. "Look at me," he said.

He called up his dad at work and told him the news. "Look

at you, Mark!" Mr. Hopper said. "When I'm down this weekend, we'll all celebrate."

Mark thought all day about how he was going to be in all honors classes in middle school. He pictured himself making even the toughest teachers smile by answering their hardest questions, and reading four-hundred-page books in one night—for fun. Maybe he and Beth could enter some sort of competition for smart brothers and sisters, and they could win lots of money. He was picturing himself and Beth being presented with a four-foot-long check on TV when he collided with his mother and her bags of groceries. "Mark—" she said with a sigh.

"Wait!" said Mark before he could get in trouble. "My schedule came today. You have to look at it." He took it out of his pocket, where he'd been holding on to it so Granpda Murray wouldn't put it somewhere where they'd never find it again, and took the groceries out of her hands so she could look at it. He wanted to see her expression, but instead he rushed out to the car and got the rest of the groceries and carried them inside in one trip. When he came back in and placed them on the counter, his mother was on the phone with the school.

"I think there might be a mistake with my son's schedule," she said.

"Mom!" Mark said. He felt very hot behind his eyes. "I can do it," he whispered. "Can I at least try?"

Mrs. Hopper gave him a puzzled look and lifted her finger to signal for him to wait. "Yes, his name is Mark Hopper, and you put him in band instead of art."

Mark rushed up and wrapped his arms around her waist. She hugged him back and bent down to kiss him on the forehead, but froze midway there. "No, I called last week and we went through this. He definitely wants art."

Ethel was on the other end of the phone. She had been there the day Mark Hopper came barging into the office, red-faced and panting, with a bicycle helmet hanging off the back of his neck and a bassoon practice book clutched in his sweaty hand. "He's changed his mind again," she murmured to Mindy, covering the mouthpiece of the phone with her hand, "and he's having his mother call to change it back." Mindy rolled her eyes and nodded knowingly, and Ethel returned to her call with Mrs. Hopper. "I will change it back to art, but this is the last time," she said. "He will get his new schedule in homeroom on the first day of school. And, Mrs. Hopper, please tell your son that the next time he takes it upon himself to speak to us in the office, he should do so politely."

Mrs. Hopper was taken aback. She couldn't imagine Mark speaking to anybody in an office of his own accord, and she certainly could not picture him being anything but polite. "I think you're mistaking my son for someone else," she said. Mark looked up at her.

"I think *you're* mistaking your son for someone else," Ethel said curtly.

Mrs. Hopper was becoming angry. "My son would never speak to anybody disrespectfully. He is a very sweet and caring boy. And *smart*," she added, smiling down at Mark.

"Oh yes, he made sure we knew *that*," Ethel said. And then, without saying anything else, she did something very impolite herself: she hung up.

Chapter 6

Mark's Locker and Mark's Homeroom

Mark Hopper and Mark Hopper both got to school early on the first day; they both wanted to make a good impression on their teachers and demonstrate that they belonged in all honors classes.

Mark packed his backpack the night before, placing six different colored binders, with matching folders, in his backpack. Each contained the note that he had printed out on labels: PROPERTY OF MARK GEOFFREY HOPPER. PRIVATE AND NONE OF YOUR BUSINESS. He didn't want anyone copying his notes or stealing his homework and auctioning off the answers.

Mark also packed his backpack the night before, though its contents were only a pad of paper, a folder, a blue pen, a black pen, and two pencils. One of the pencils said PROPERTY OF MARK GEOFFREY HOPPER. Grandpa Murray had had those printed up and gave them to Mark when he started kindergarten. Mark was always lending them out, so he had only one left, and he considered it his lucky pencil. He had also written MARK HOPPER nice and big in permanent marker all over his folder. Beth had suggested he put his name on it so someone could return it to him in case it got lost. When Mark proudly showed her how he'd made his name stretch the whole folder, she stifled laughter and said that that wasn't quite what she had in mind, but it definitely could not be mistaken for anybody else's.

Mark Hopper got to school so early that there was hardly anybody else in the hallway. Only a few students were hanging out by the front doors, looking at their watches and checking their outfits and waiting for their friends to arrive. Mark passed a few kids he knew from elementary school on his way to his locker. "Hey, Steve-o," he said to Steve Dobbs, whom he hadn't spoken to since second grade. "Don't have time to compare schedules, but don't worry. We might be in some classes together if you're in all honors." He slapped Steve on the back and continued on, looking for locker 322. He found it on the first floor, right near a girls' bathroom. He stuck out his tongue in concentration while turning the combination. "Thirty-six . . ." he mumbled. "Turn right two times . . . four . . . turn left to eighteen . . . and . . . presto!" The lock opened with a satisfying *click*. "Bam!" Mark shouted. A girl with long black hair who was at a locker down the hall turned and gave him a strange look. "How's yours coming? I got mine on the first try, so if you need help just let me know," Mark shouted down at her.

She stared at him as though he was from Neptune, then turned back to her locker.

Mark knelt down and unzipped his backpack. He took out a

box that contained special locker shelves he had had his mother purchase. By the time he had fitted the shelves and placed his afternoon binders on them, a few more students were arriving and chatting. He looked around for Jasmina, who had locker 326, but didn't see her. He did see Frank Stucco, however, and he looked like he'd put on some weight over the summer. Not wanting Frank to see him, Mark closed up his locker and sauntered in the other direction. He passed the dark-haired girl, who was now leaning against a closed locker and chatting to a few other girls. "How'd it go with your locker?" Mark asked.

All of the girls looked at him blankly.

"I'm Mark Hopper," he said.

The girls looked at one another, each wondering which of them knew him. Finally, one of them spoke. "I'm Laurie," she said between bites on her nails.

"Do you have homeroom now?" asked the dark-haired girl, who decided to try to be friendly.

"Duh," Mark said. He gave her his why-would-you-bother-saying-something-so-useless expression that he practiced on his sister daily. "Are you guys in all honors classes?"

Laurie nearly choked on the fingernail she was chewing. "What? Who cares?" she asked. The other girls crossed their arms and gave one another looks. One of them rolled her eyes and became very involved in looking through her book bag.

"Well, I am," Mark said. "See you around." As he walked away, he heard the girls laughing, and he could have sworn he heard one of them say something about meeting all the freaks. Well, he didn't want to be friends with people who weren't open to meeting new people anyway.

• • •

In the meantime, Mark Hopper arrived at Ivy Road with his eyes wide as ever. The school was so big, and the hallways were wide and crowded with students who were hugging and talking and comparing summer stories. He wished he had Sammy by his side, at least to help him find his locker and sit with at lunch. Reminding himself that most the sixth graders knew hardly anyone helped him feel a bit more confident. He hoped his teachers wouldn't be harsh about people being late; looking around the maze of hallways, he was sure it would take him at least a week to get used to where to go. A big kid in an Ivy Road Roadrunners jacket bumped into him. "Watch it, little guy," he said. Mark apologized and stared after him, unsure of what to do. He turned in a complete circle, watching students open their lockers and put their jackets and some notebooks inside. That was it: he should find his locker. He took out a crumpled piece of paper from his pocket. Locker 322. He tried to get a look at the number on a locker nearby but his view was obstructed by a passing group of girls in matching cheerleader outfits: short skirts and tight tops with the letters *I* and *R* printed across them. He looked at the place on his wrist where a watch should have been. Did he have time to try to find his locker, or should he just try to find his homeroom? Maybe he should ask someone for the time. A girl who looked about his age was consulting a sheet of paper right near him. She had her long black hair in hundreds of tiny braids. "Excuse me," Mark said.

The girl turned and smiled at him. Her braids swished. "You look lost," she said.

"I'm new," Mark said. He felt himself turning red.

"Me too. All the sixth graders are." She said it kindly. "Have you found your locker yet?"

"No. Do you have any idea where number 322 might be?"

The girl's smile became a grin. "I think it should be right near mine. I'm 326. I'm Jasmina," she said. "Let's go this way."

Mark walked alongside her. "Thanks," Mark said. "My name's Mark."

"Huh," said Jasmina. "There's another kid named Mark whose locker is right near ours, too. I think he's number 322."

"I'm 322," Mark said.

"Oh yeah," said Jasmina. "Maybe he's 323 or something. Hey! All right. Here it is. Well, here's 326 anyway. Three twenty-two must be close."

Mark thanked her and went one panel over to locker 322. He knelt down and entered the combination: 36–4–18. The lock opened without a problem and Mark let out a grateful sigh, even though he didn't really have anything to put in it. When he pulled open the door, however, his mouth dropped open. His locker was equipped with fancy shelves. He looked around to see if anybody else had shelves, but he couldn't tell. On the shelves, however, were three binders, each a different color. He didn't remember anything saying he had to share a locker. Could they have mistakenly assigned this locker to two people? Though he felt like he was snooping around someone's room, he reached for one of the binders. "Holy . . ." he muttered. On the cover was a printed sticker that said PROPERTY OF MARK GEOFFREY HOPPER. PRIVATE AND NONE OF YOUR BUSINESS. Was this a joke? He tried to look around to see if anybody else had binders labeled especially for them in their lockers. He wanted to ask someone, but what if giving students personalized binders on the first day was standard ritual at Ivy Road? Though his were awfully mean-spirited. And if no one else *did* find personalized binders in their lockers, then he'd really sound weird. If they were there on purpose, then that meant he'd need them for class, and he should put some in his backpack. But if it was some sort of mistake, then he should probably leave them there. But they did say his name on them—his *full* name, with his middle name spelled correctly and everything. Who else's could they be? He carefully took the black one off its shelf and stuck it in his backpack.

"Hey!"

Mark, startled, slammed his locker door closed and whirled around.

Jasmina laughed. "Sorry," she said. "I didn't mean to scare you. What homeroom are you in?"

"Um," Mark said, still trying to figure out the binder mystery and recover from being jolted out of his thought process.

"I figured that since our lockers are close we might have the same homeroom. I'm in room 140."

Mark took out the crumpled schedule from his pocket. Sure enough, he was in room 140 as well.

"Cool!" said his new friend. "Want to compare the rest of our schedules?"

"We could," Mark said, "but it'd kind of be a waste. They messed up my schedule, so I'm getting a new one in homeroom. It'll probably be all different."

"Oh, well, let's compare once you get your new one, then. But come on, homeroom's almost starting."

Mark felt his ears turning red as he walked alongside Jasmina toward homeroom.

In the meantime, Mark Hopper had found his homeroom, room 140, and introduced himself to the teacher, Mrs. Frances. Mrs. Frances had bright orange hair, crunchy-looking red lipstick, and drawn-on eyebrows. When Mark introduced himself and shook her hand, Mrs. Frances handed him Mark Hopper's new schedule.

"What is this?" Mark asked.

"There was a mistake with your schedule, and this is your new one. That's what the office told me."

Mark looked at it through tight eyelids. His face grew red and his breath heavy. "Art?" he said through gritted teeth. "They put me back in art?"

"Is there a problem?" Mrs. Frances asked. Her smiling red lips angered Mark even more.

"Yes, there's a problem," he said. "I need to go to the office and correct this."

Mrs. Frances wrote him a pass.

Mark stormed away, barreling through the students entering the room and knocking one of them into the door frame.

"Whoa, hey!" the boy said.

"Get over it," Mark shot back. He passed Jasmina and Mark Hopper. "Where are you going?" Jasmina called.

"They screwed up my schedule again!" Mark called back.

Jasmina shook her head. "I know him," she told the Mark next to her. "He's always like that."

"Really?" said Mark, his eyes round as usual.

"Always."

The two walked into Mrs. Frances's room. About twenty

students were there, standing near desks. A few were talking quietly, but most of them were just looking around. Mark and Jasmina went to neighboring desks and started to sit down.

"Don't sit down!" yelled Mrs. Frances.

Mark and Jasmina stopped themselves mid-sit. She had said it with such urgency that Mark was glad he hadn't sat yet—maybe the chair would have collapsed.

"I'm going to assign you seats," Mrs. Frances said more calmly.

"Sheesh," whispered Jasmina. "I thought the seats were covered in slime or something."

The bell sounded and the few students who had been talking abruptly became silent. Mark stood by the chair on which he'd almost sat, staring at Mrs. Frances with curiosity.

"Good morning!" Mrs. Frances sang. "Welcome back! I hope you had a nice summer. Eighth grade will be tough, but it will also be fun."

All of the students—sixth graders—looked around anxiously as though trying to gauge the age of the others and determine if the mistake was hers or theirs. None were brave enough to ask. Mrs. Frances slowly turned her whole body to show each part of the classroom her broad smile. Her teeth were smeared with lipstick. "We are going to sit alphabetically. Please take a seat when I call your name." She rotated with her smile once more before beginning: "Halpern, Julie." Julie Halpern took the first seat. The list continued all through the *H*s, students filing into their seats one by one. The process took a long time because as each student sat down, Mrs. Frances personally welcomed him or her to the eighth grade.

When Mrs. Frances called Max Hooper, Mark Hopper thought

it might be a mistake, and moved to sit down. But Max Hooper, a short, squat boy with sharply cut blond hair, stared at him with his eyebrows raised. "Are you Max Hooper?" Max asked.

"Oh, sorry," said Mark Hopper. "I'm—"

"No problem, dude," said Max Hooper. He sat in the seat.

All of the other students laughed, and Mark felt his ears turning red for the second time that morning. They must have thought he was stupid, not knowing his own name. But once Mrs. Frances called Mark Hopper, they would understand what the confusion was.

"Horace, Jasmina," said Mrs. Frances.

Jasmina began to sit down in the seat behind Max Hooper.

"Don't sit down!" shouted Mrs. Frances.

Jasmina jumped up.

"Please skip that seat," Mrs. Frances said calmly. "That student is currently working out his schedule trouble."

"Sheesh," Jasmina whispered. "She has got to stop doing that."

Mark's mind was racing. Mrs. Frances had skipped him. In alphabetical order, Hopper should come between Hooper and Horace. He ran through the alphabet silently to make sure.

Mrs. Frances just finished calling out the names, all the way through Jacobson, Katherine, when the bell rang to end homeroom. Everyone rose from their newly assigned seats and started heading out. Except for Mark—he had not been assigned a seat at all. Jasmina smiled at him before leaving. "This lady's a kook," she said. "She doesn't know what she's talking about."

"I hope so," said Mark. "I need my new schedule, too."

"I'd better run," said Jasmina. "But good luck and welcome to the eighth grade!"

Mark was too nervous to laugh. He approached Mrs. Frances's desk.

"Yes?" she said.

"Hi, um. You didn't call me. I'm Mark Hopper."

Mrs. Frances looked at him cockeyed for a moment before smiling. "Of course," she said. "How did it go?"

"What?" said Mark. Remembering his manners, he quickly corrected himself and said, "Excuse me?"

"With your schedule?"

"Um, that's what I came to ask you about. There was a mistake with my schedule and I need a new one."

"Speak up, please. I can barely hear you."

"There was a mistake with my schedule. I'm supposed to get a new one."

"So why did you leave the office?"

"What?" Mark was more confused than ever. Even though his last name fit perfectly in room 140, maybe he had come to the wrong homeroom. "Am I supposed to be in this homeroom? You didn't call me."

Mrs. Frances smiled. "I didn't call you because I knew you were in the office. But you are in this homeroom." She took out the roster and pointed to the line that read "Hopper, Mark Geoffrey."

Mark stared at the roster for a full ten seconds before Mrs. Frances said, "Off to first period, Mark. You only get three minutes to change classrooms." Then she chuckled and shook her head. "Silly me; you know how middle school works. You are in eighth grade!"

Chapter 7

Mark Meets Mark

"I want to talk to your supervisor!" Mark Hopper bellowed.

Ethel sat with her shoulders squared and her lips pursed. Her eyes glowered at Mark over her square reading glasses. "For the last time," she said in a clipped voice. "You will speak to *me*, young man. And I will only listen if you speak calmly, not if you yell."

"I am speaking calmly!" Mark yelled. "And since you won't listen, then I'll speak to someone above you. The principal!"

Ethel looked right past him. "Next student, please. What can I help you with?"

Mark took a loud step aside and stood by the corner of Ethel's desk. His breathing was heavy and his face was hot. The schedule with art on it was clutched between his sweaty fingers. He told himself to calm down; he would get what he wanted only if he was thinking clearly enough to present his points.

After a few deep breaths he felt more collected. But he didn't want Ethel to think he wasn't still angry or, worse, that she had won. So he glared at her with his most intense, I'm-going-to-make-you-sorry-you-ever-crossed-me glare that he occasionally practiced in front of the mirror at night.

Mark Hopper entered the office and took a place in the line. He saw the boy who had rushed past him and Jasmina earlier, shouting about his schedule—the one Jasmina knew—simmering by the front and staring at the secretary with a face so fierce it could be emitting invisible but deadly laser beams. Mark was amazed. He wondered what the problem with his schedule was. It must be something really serious if it had gotten him so worked up.

The other students spoke to the secretary one by one while Mark stood off to the side, making a show of his impatience. Twice, he looked at his wrist to signal that he had been waiting a long time, but the effect was weakened by the fact that he wasn't wearing a watch.

Mark Hopper didn't mind waiting about five minutes for his turn; it gave him time to plan out and practice what he was going to say. When he finally stepped forward, the angry kid crossed in front of Ethel and protested. "I've been waiting a really long time now," he said.

"Yes, thank you for your patience," said Ethel sweetly. "Just let me help this young man and then it will be your turn."

Mark let out a long, loud sigh but stepped aside once more.

Mark Hopper approached the desk cautiously. "Sorry," he said to Mark. "This shouldn't take too long."

Mark responded with a sneer that Mark interpreted as an attempt at a smile.

"I need to talk to you about my schedule," he said, trying to remember the way he had practiced it in his head. "My name is Mark Hopper."

"What?" said Ethel.

"What?" said Mark.

"What?" said Mark. "I mean, excuse me?"

"Is this a joke?" said Ethel, crossing her arms.

Mark crossed his arms, too.

Mark became very nervous. "No," he said, forgetting everything he had planned in an instant. "There was, um, a problem with my schedule, and um . . ."

Ethel placed her hands on her desk and looked at both Marks over her glasses. "This is not funny, boys," she said severely.

"Me?" shouted Mark Hopper, his five minutes of calming himself down flying out the window in under one second. "Who put you up to this?" he snapped to Mark.

"I really don't know what you're talking about," Mark said quietly.

Mark Hopper began pacing the room, waving the sweat-covered, crumpled schedule. "Ha-ha. Mark Hopper has a schedule problem and needs to go to the office. Wouldn't it be funny if someone went to pretend to be him to make fun of him?"

Mark looked at Mark with round eyes. He would have been afraid if he hadn't been so confused.

"Who put you up to this?" Mark said in a low voice. "Frank Stucco? Pete Dale?"

"No," said Mark.

"Was it my sister?" Mark asked, his voice rising.

Ethel cleared her throat. "I don't want to have to send both of you boys to the principal on the first day of school," she said, though her tone of voice suggested that she did. "Is there really even a problem with your schedule at all?"

"Yes," said both Marks at the same time, though one much louder than the other.

"My schedule has art on it instead of band. Again."

"My schedule should have art, but it's all wrong. I was supposed to get a new one in homeroom."

"All right," said Ethel. "I remember speaking with your mother," she said to the irate Mark, "and she told me that you were one hundred percent sure that you wanted art."

The wide-eyed Mark became even wider-eyed. "My mom spoke to someone and said that *I* definitely wanted art, too."

"So your mom is in on this, too?" shouted Mark. "Let's all make fun of Mark Hopper."

"But I am Mark Hopper."

Mark huffed.

Ethel looked from Mark Hopper to Mark Hopper and back to Mark Hopper. A few of the other secretaries and office staff had stopped working or emerged from the back of the office to watch the scene. "He seems like the real Mark Hopper to me," one whispered to another, who shook her head and whispered that she thought the opposite.

Mindy, who'd been listening from her desk nearby, got up and stood by Ethel. She logged in to the computer and brought up Mark's information. "Mark Geoffrey Hopper," she said.

"Yes," said Mark.

"Hi," said Mark.

"How do you spell Geoffrey?" Mindy said.

While Mark said, *"G-E-O-F-F-R-E-Y,"* Mark said, "The dumb way, with a *G*."

"Which of you has a sister named Beth?" tried Mindy, smiling at her genius.

"Me," said Mark, sticking his nose in the air.

"I do," said Mark, amazed that they knew his sister's name.

"Do you guys have ID? A driver's license?" asked Mindy, becoming exasperated.

"I'm eleven," said Mark. He gave her his I'm-much-smarter-than-you'll-ever-be look that he practiced every time someone said something stupid.

"I assume you both live on Crown Road?" said Ethel, squinting at the computer screen.

"I live on Crown Road," said Mark.

Everyone waited in silence for Mark to say that he did, too. But he finally said, "I don't live on Crown Road."

"Aha!" said Ethel. Then her smiled faded. She wasn't sure what she had proved.

Mindy looked at the computer. "When is your birthday?" she asked the Mark who lived on Crown Road. The file said March 10.

"April fourth," replied Mark.

Mindy sighed.

"My birthday is March tenth!" yelled the Mark who did not live on Crown Road.

"Aha!" said Mindy. Then she and Ethel looked at each other. They were even more confused.

"Look," said Mark. He waved his arms to get everyone's attention. "I think you are all the dumbest people alive. Either this guy is playing a really big joke on all of us, or we are both named Mark Geoffrey Hopper."

Mark's eyes became round as he realized that that actually

made sense. That would explain why band was on his schedule and why binders with his name on them were in his locker. The binders! He opened his backpack and took out the folder on which he'd written his name in big, sprawling letters. "This is mine," he said. Then he took out one of the binders he had taken from his locker that said PROPERTY OF MARK GEOFFREY HOPPER. PRIVATE AND NONE OF YOUR BUSINESS. "Is this yours?" he asked Mark.

"Yeah!" said Mark. He grabbed it and examined it for damage. Then he took out a matching one from his backpack and showed it to the office staff. "We're both Mark Hopper," Mark said to the staff in his most uppity voice. "But you only have one Mark Hopper registered." He shook his head and muttered, "Morons."

The other Mark felt his ears turn red at his namesake's rudeness. "I'm sorry," he stammered. Then he faced Mark with his eyes wide and round. He said, "I can't believe we have the exact same name."

Mark huffed. He said, "I can't believe you stole my binder."

Chapter **8**

Mark Ruins
Mark's Reputation

"This other Mark Hopper is ruining my reputation," Mark said to his sister that night.

Beth snorted. She took a piece of the gum she was chewing and stretched it out from her mouth, twirling it around and around her finger. "How can he be ruining your reputation when he just got there?" she asked as she twirled.

"People already think I'm stupid for getting so worked up about a schedule that didn't even belong to me."

"People think you're stupid anyway," Beth said.

"Shut up," said Mark. "People know *I'm* not stupid. But who knows about this other Mark? He's probably really stupid. He'll probably fail all of his classes and then people will say, 'Oh, Mark Hopper is pretty dumb,' and other people will think they're talking about me."

Beth shook her gum-covered finger at her brother. "You're always thinking of yourself," she scolded. "Think about this poor other guy named Mark Hopper. People are probably saying, 'Mark Hopper is really ugly,' and other people will they think they mean him!"

Mark lifted a corner of his mouth. "Ha. Ha."

"Yes," continued Beth, examining the gum and looking under the couch for a place to put it. "I think I like this other Mark."

"You haven't even met him."

"Doesn't matter. I already know I like him more than you. Now when I say I have a brother named Mark, maybe people will think it's him."

"You're a jerk."

"Just kidding, baby brother," Beth said. She stroked her gum-covered finger along Mark's cheek.

"Ugh, gross!" Mark shouted. He jumped off the couch and froze a few feet away with a scary thought. He had been looking forward for years to being old enough to enter a statewide middle school competition called the Mastermind tournament. Mark was sure he could win, even though he was only in sixth grade. He spent many nights dreaming about winning the tournament and having everyone praise his brilliance until he had to insist, halfheartedly, that they stop. But this other Mark Hopper could screw it all up.

"What if he enters the Mastermind tournament?" Mark said to Beth, envisioning the other Mark being presented the Mastermind trophy and staring at it with surprised eyes. "If our applications get mixed up, he'll cancel out all of my hard work!"

"Hmm," said Beth. She tapped her gummy finger against her lips in thought. "I think you need to find out more about this Mark Geoffrey Hopper guy before getting so worked up. And then—once you know what you need to watch out for with him—do whatever you need to to take care of it."

"That's actually a pretty smart idea." Mark blurted out. Upon seeing his sister's smirk, he quickly added, "Of course I thought of it myself five seconds before you did. You just said it first."

Beth rolled her eyes.

"But it still is pretty smart," Mark granted her.

She shrugged. "I'm high-school-smart now. That means I'm mature." And with that, she stuck her gum-covered finger into Mark's ear.

Chapter 9

Mark Ruins
Mark's Reputation

"This other Mark Hopper is giving me a bad reputation," Mark explained to Beth and Grandpa Murray later.

"Everyone is new," Beth reasoned. "So there shouldn't be too many people who know about him."

"You don't understand," Mark said. "This guy is really something. People who don't know about him now will in a few days. And I bet they won't like him."

"How much would you bet?" asked Grandpa Murray. He was always up for a bet.

"Everything," Mark said. "Everything I own. Plus one million dollars."

Grandpa Murray let out a low whistle. "I'm not taking that bet."

Mark nodded solemnly. "He's that bad."

"I don't advocate violence," Grandpa Murray said, "but I think you should pop him one." He punched one hand with the other.

"Oh, come on, Grandpa," said Beth. "How will that help?"

"It'll make Mark known as the *tough* Mark Hopper."

"But Mark isn't tough."

"Sure he is. He just *looks* weak so bullies don't know what they have coming."

"No, I'm not tough," Mark said, patting Grandpa Murray on the shoulder. "And even if I was, what if people got it messed up and thought the other Mark beat *me* up?" Mark's eyes became wide. "What if he does beat me up because I took his binder?"

Beth raised one eyebrow. "That's ridiculous. The binder had your name on it. It was an honest mistake. He would have done the same if he had found your binders in his locker. Besides, from what you said, it sounds like he doesn't fight with anything but his mouth."

"His big, fat mouth," Mark mumbled.

"Mark," Grandpa Murray whispered. When Mark looked, he punched his fist into his hand again.

"Grandpa!" Beth said. She gave Mark a half-full smile. "Don't stress about him. At least not yet. I'm sure people will realize you two are nothing alike. Or maybe he was just high-strung because it was the first day and there were problems."

Mark returned her smile with a half-empty one. "On his binder he wrote 'private and none of your business.'"

"All I'm saying is maybe he's not really *that* bad. Wait and see."

"I guess I'd better get to my homework," Mark said.

"Do you have a lot?" Beth asked.

"Yeah!" complained Mark.

"I have a lot, too!" Beth sighed and said dreamily, "I love my new school!"

Grandpa Murray shook his head. "I love you, Beth," he said. "But you're really weird."

Mark Scopes Out Mark

For the next couple of weeks the two Mark Hoppers scoped each other out, which was not too difficult because, though they were finally given individual schedules, they had two classes together in the morning, plus homeroom. In the afternoon they were in separate classes until seventh period, when they would come together in gym class and each regard the other based on what he had heard about his behavior throughout the afternoon. Mark would usually feel pretty down by seventh period—he would have overheard some boys imitating Mark's smarmy way of answering questions in class or he'd have walked into computer class sixth period and seen Mark still there from fifth period, kissing up to the teacher while the other kids made fun of him. His mood wasn't helped by the fact that the other Mark would glare at him and sigh audibly every time he ran a lap or threw a ball. He made a conscious effort to try to like Mark, or at least not hate him, though Mark made no such effort with Mark. Nothing Mark said or did was acceptable to Mark, and vice versa, and they both hated thinking that everyone else thought of them in terms of the other.

And everyone did confuse them because it was so confusing. Mrs. Frances, who had them both in her homeroom, plus Max Hooper, just couldn't get it. Teachers who arranged their students alphabetically had an especially hard time because it meant that Mark and Mark would be sitting right behind each other. But it didn't even help when teachers sat them apart.

For example, in social studies one day, Mr. Rocco asked the class if they knew what the ancient Egyptians used the pyramids for. Both Marks raised their hands.

"Yes, Mark," said Mr. Rocco, pointing to the Mark on the right side of the classroom near the windows.

"The mummies of the dead pharaohs," said the Mark sitting on the left side of the room by the door.

"I called on the other Mark."

"Oh, sorry." Mark smiled sweetly, though his sweet smile looked more like a twisted smirk. He knew perfectly well that Mr. Rocco had called on the other Mark, but he wanted Mr. Rocco to know that he knew the answer, and he wanted to answer before the other Mark could get it wrong and embarrass them both.

Mr. Rocco sighed. "Mark?" he said to the other.

Mark's shoulders dropped. "That's what I was going to say," he said. "It's where they put the mummies." He hoped Mr. Rocco knew that he had really known the answer before the other Mark had said it.

"That's correct," said Mr. Rocco. "Please, Mark," he said to the one who deserved the reprimand, "don't speak out of turn."

Mark waited a few seconds before looking up from his notebook. "Oh!" he said, smiling again. "Do you mean me-Mark? It's just so confusing."

The rest of the class snickered. The other Mark sank into his seat, wondering if an eleven-year-old could legally change his name.

When Miss Payley handed back quizzes in math, she called the two Marks up to her desk so that they could figure out whose was whose. Mark recognized his handwriting instantly, but before he could take his quiz and quietly go back to his desk, the other Mark grabbed his own and held it up. "This one is mine, Miss Payley," he said loudly enough for the entire class—maybe even the entire school, Mark thought—to hear. "*I* got a hundred. The *other* Mark got a seventy-two and drew a stupid little cartoon in the corner of the paper."

Mark felt his ears turn bright red and stared at Mark with his wide blue eyes.

"Mark!" Miss Payley said sternly. "We don't compare grades in this class. Especially not aloud."

Mark shrugged and crossed his arms. "Sorry." He knew it wasn't exactly nice to say things like that, but how else could he make it clear that he was the smart Mark? He was also kind of glad no one could see Mark's drawing, which was actually a very good sketch of a hand holding a pencil. But it was still stupid to draw it on a math test, Mark thought. It was things like that that soiled the name Mark Hopper.

Miss Payley told him to come talk to her after school, and

Mark stomped back to his desk with his face bright red. This other Mark was definitely ruining everything for him. He had *never* gotten detention before he appeared. He wondered if an eleven-year-old could legally change his name. He'd change it to something distinct, like Einstein. Einstein Hopper—how perfect would that be?

The other Mark went back to his desk with his wide eyes glued to the floor. He couldn't believe how much the other Mark was ruining everything for him. Why was he being so mean? His seventy-two on the math quiz didn't help his mood, either. Beth had helped him study and everything. He flipped to the back of the quiz, taking in all of the red marks, and he found a note from Miss Payley: "Please come talk to me after school." His mood sank even further. He looked at the quick sketch he had drawn while trying to figure out one of the word problems. It wasn't stupid, he wondered, was it?

He felt something hit him in the back of the head. He looked around. A boy named Jonathan was grinning at him and pointing at the floor. There was a piece of paper folded into a tight triangle. Mark pointed at himself with wide eyes, and Jonathan nodded. Mark checked to see that Miss Payley wasn't looking before he picked up the note. "The Cool Mark Hopper" was written on the outside in spiky handwriting. He felt his ears turn red once more as he carefully unfolded it. "Stinks you have to have the same name as that jerk!" the note read. Mark turned around and nodded at Jonathan, who laughed in response.

"What's funny?" asked Miss Payley.

Mark turned back around to pay attention. For the first time since he found out about him, he thought that this other Mark might actually be good for something.

. . .

After class, Jonathan caught up to Mark. "Did you go to elementary school with that other Mark, too?" he asked.

"No," said Mark. "I just moved to Greenburgh this summer."

Jonathan patted him on the back. "Aren't you in art eighth period?"

"Yeah," said Mark.

"Are you going to join the art club?"

"Yeah!" said Mark, his eyes wide. Then, trying to pull back his enthusiasm, he shrugged. "Are you in it?"

"I'm going to the meeting after school to see what it's all about."

"I want to go," Mark said, thinking about his meeting with Miss Payley and feeling his mood dampen again. "But I might be kind of late, and I don't know how long it's going to last."

"Well, I'm definitely going, so I can let you know what happens and sign you up. Do you have lunch now?"

"Yeah."

"Me, too. Let's go."

Ashamed at having gotten detention, Mark was mostly quiet the rest of the day. He didn't raise his hand once during computers, and he barely spoke at all while doing group work in science—though strangely enough, the other kids in the group seemed to like him more for it. One of them, a pretty girl he thought was named Julia—though maybe it was Julie or Maria—even asked him if everything was okay. "Of course everything's okay! Mind your own business," Mark snapped back at her. She held up her hands in surrender and walked away, and Mark rolled his eyes.

He sat at Jasmina's lunch table, like he did every day. As he ate his turkey sandwich, he listened to the conversations around him and wondered how all of these people seemed to have so many new friends already. Well, he had Jasmina. And he had the Mastermind tournament to plan for. It was good that he didn't have more than one friend yet, he reasoned. Otherwise he wouldn't be able to prepare fully because he'd be so busy socializing.

He heard a familiar voice from a few tables away. It was the other Mark Hopper talking easily to a group of boys. He was showing them what seemed to be a drawing. Mark pretended to stretch and looked over. It was a complicated sketch of an old man. Mark figured he must have traced it—no one in sixth grade could draw that well—but the other boys seemed to be impressed anyway. If that wasn't bad enough, after Mark finished saying something, the other boys laughed and responded. The other Mark Hopper had friends.

"Mark." Jasmina snapped her fingers in front of Mark's face. "Earth to Mark."

"What?" Mark said.

"What is wrong with you today? Did you do badly on that math test or something?"

"Of course not," Mark said sharply. "I have to stay after school for a little today. Can you wait to walk home?"

Jasmina shook her head and her braids clicked together. "Nope," she said. "I'm going to Kylie's house after school."

Mark snorted. "Fine," he said. He took another bite of his sandwich and chewed it angrily.

Jasmina stared at him with her eyebrows raised. "Timmy will be home this afternoon. I'm sure he'll want to hang out with you."

"I don't want to play with your stupid six-year-old brother," Mark said, spewing turkey and bread.

"Suit yourself." Jasmina shrugged, turned away from him, and starting chatting with Kylie.

"I'm going to finish my lunch in the library," Mark said to no one in particular. He packed up and left, making sure to go by Mark's table and look purposely straight ahead as he passed, as though he didn't even notice Mark was there.

Chapter 11

Mark's Punishment

The Mark who needed to speak to Miss Payley about his poor test grade would normally have put off their meeting as long as possible. He would have dawdled at his locker, turning the lock slowly and pausing on each number for a few seconds before leisurely selecting the books he'd need for homework and placing them carefully side by side in his backpack. Then he'd have walked at a turtle's pace all the way around the square-shaped building so as to take the longest path to Miss Payley's room, probably stopping in the boys' bathroom—and moving at the same snail-like speed in there—on the way. But today he rushed straight over from art to get it over with as soon as possible. Partly he wanted to be done with it quickly so that he wouldn't have to worry about it anymore, and partly he wanted to finish in time to go to the art club meeting, since Jonathan was saving him a seat. But mostly he wanted to be in and out before the other Mark Hopper arrived for his detention. He was so relieved to find only Miss Payley there when he arrived that he realized he was more upset about the other Mark than about his grades.

"Mark," said Miss Payley. "What happened on that quiz?"

He took out his test so quickly he almost ripped the paper. "I don't know," he whispered, his large blue eyes apologetic. "I think I'm just off to a shaky start, but I will get better. I'm trying."

"I understand." Miss Payley smiled. "It is a big adjustment from elementary school to middle school."

Mark nodded. She sounded like his mom. It is a big adjustment, she'd said, and you're going to have to work very hard, especially in honors classes. He was not looking forward to showing the test to his mom that night. "I think I will definitely do better next time," he promised. "My sister is going to help me. She's really smart."

"Beth?" asked Miss Payley.

"Yeah," said Mark, wondering if Miss Payley was thinking of his sister or the other Beth Hopper, and if the other Beth Hopper was as awful as her terrible, life-ruining brother.

"In class," Miss Payley said gently, "do I go too quickly for you sometimes?"

Mark didn't know how to answer. If he confessed that she did, she might suggest that he move down into the regular class. But maybe she thought she was going too quickly for everyone, and she wanted to know so that she could slow down. "A little," Mark said, compromising. "Sometimes."

At that moment the other Mark entered the room. "Miss Payley, I want to apologize," he announced loudly.

Miss Payley turned. "One moment, Mark. We're talking here. Take a seat."

Mark slumped down into a desk. Each Mark tried to avoid looking at the other.

Miss Payley paused and then turned to the Mark who had just walked in. "All right. I think you should apologize," she said to him.

"I'm sorry," he said.

"And to Mark."

"I'm sorry, Mark," Mark grumbled.

"For . . ." Miss Payley prompted.

"For announcing your grade to the class, especially because it was a bad grade."

"And . . ." continued Miss Payley.

"And?"

"And . . ."

"And it wasn't a nice thing to do? Which is why I'm sorry. And I hope you do better on the next test?"

"Thanks," mumbled the Mark who just wanted to get to art club.

"Thank you," said Miss Payley. "Tomorrow you will apologize to the rest of the class."

Mark almost argued with her because what he just did was bad enough—*How many freaking times did he need to apologize?*—but decided to keep quiet. He tightened his lips and crossed his arms.

Miss Payley turned back to the other Mark, who was tracing the outline of the floor tiles with his foot. "This is going to be a fast-moving class, Mark," she said to him. "I know this is only the very beginning, but I don't want you to fall behind."

"I won't," promised Mark.

"Well, just in case," Miss Payley continued, "I think it might be a good idea to set you up with a study partner. That way you can be sure to keep up right from the start. I think that's a better idea than waiting a few weeks and seeing how it goes, because then it might be harder to catch up."

Mark's eyes widened at the idea. Maybe Jonathan could be his study partner. Then they would definitely become friends. Or maybe Jasmina—she seemed really nice and smart, and he was pretty sure she had Miss Payley a different period. "Okay," Mark said. "I'll do that."

"Great," said Miss Payley. "Mark," she said to the other Mark. "Putting your behavior this morning aside for a moment, you really seem to be catching on to the work quickly . . ."

"Thank you, Miss Payley," called Mark as he started out the door.

"Wait!" said Miss Payley. "Hold on one second, Mark. Mark, I would really like it if you and Mark would be study partners."

Both Marks froze.

"Excuse me?"

"What?"

"Yes, I think you two will work wonderfully together," Miss Payley said with a playful smile.

Mark thought he'd work better with someone he actually wanted to like.

Mark thought he'd work better with a dead dog.

"You can have your first study session tomorrow afternoon. You can use this room."

"Um—"

"But—"

"That's all, Mark Hoppers," Miss Payley said. She put on her jacket and picked up her bag. "I'll see you tomorrow," she said.

The two Marks stared at each other—one seething with anger and one consumed with worry—but they both could have sworn that from the corner of their eye they saw Miss Payley do a little jig on her way out the door.

Chapter 12

The Trouble with the Mastermind Tournament

That night, Mark made a list:

Reasons I cannot be Mark Hopper's study partner

1. I am doing perfectly in math (and every other class) so far, so I don't need a study partner.
2. Mark needs so much help that it will take time away from my homework and my grades might drop.
3. We have the same name and it could get confusing.
4. I maybe want to join debate club and then I will not have time to meet him after school.
5. I need time to prepare for the Mastermind tournament.

Then, just so it didn't seem like he was complaining about something that could not be changed, he made another list:

Alternate solutions for the other Mark Hopper
1. Get him a different study partner.
2. Put him in regular math.
3. **Let him move back to wherever he came from.**

His handwriting got heavy and messier while writing that last suggestion, and by the end of the sentence, it was so heavy that his period made a hole in the paper. He knew he couldn't show the list to Miss Payley with that suggestion on it, but writing it did make him feel better. So did scribbling it out quickly and wildly. When he took out a fresh piece of paper to copy the list over, he felt a bit calmer. If he presented his case rationally and reasonably, he was sure to make Miss Payley understand. He would even present it after class when the other Mark had left already, so as not to hurt his feelings. That would show Miss Payley that he was a caring person.

When he finished double-checking his math homework (it was perfect as usual, but he figured his case would be stronger if it was extra perfect), Mark took out the Mastermind tournament rules. Beth had brought home the information last year but wrapped her gum in it and dumped it in the kitchen garbage bin with a "yeah, right." Mark had taken it out of the trash, smoothed out the pages, removed the gum and food particles stuck to it, and put it in his desk. He'd been studying the rules and planning ever since.

He looked at the components of the competition and the notes he'd been keeping beneath each item:

1. Copies of all middle school report cards (copy
    of fifth-grade report card for sixth graders)
    and a current transcript.
    I have all A's!
    Status: Copy of fifth-grade report card in frame
    on my wall (make another copy?)

2. An essay, 2-4 pages long, on your goals for high
    school and beyond, and how you plan to achieve
    them.
    Easy!
    Status: 3 possible drafts written with a 9th grade
    vocabulary, at least.

3. Evidence of artistic or athletic talent. Evi-
    dence of talent in two areas is welcome.
    Status: Record professional CD of bassoon solo.

4. A public speech on current events (finalists
    only).
    Easy!
    Status: I am a master of public speaking.
    (Don't really need to prepare.)

5. An interview with the Mastermind judges (final-
    ists only).
    Easy!
    Status: Found list of common questions online. I will
    blow them away.

When he got to the bottom, his eyes traveled back up to item three. He was a great bassoon player, but it was that second note that always worried him: "Evidence of talent in two areas is welcome." That meant he *could* just send a CD of himself playing the bassoon, but if he wanted to win, he needed something else, too. He thought about singing a song on the CD, but decided that was kind of a cheesy idea; besides, what song would he sing? He considered taking opera-singing lessons. He also considered including his certificate that said he did ten chin-ups for the presidential fitness test in fifth grade. He could easily take that out of its frame and photocopy it. But that wasn't really Mastermind material. His mind drifted to the drawing the other Mark was showing his friends at lunch and the sketch on his math test. Even though Mark thought art was for people who weren't good enough to play instruments, and even though he was sure the other Mark must have traced the really good drawing, he wished just for a second that he had something like that to submit with his name on it.

"Mark! Your father is on the phone!"

Mark forgot about the other Mark instantaneously. He jumped up from his desk and barreled down the stairs. His parents had separated a few months ago, and his father had only called three times since. He hadn't visited at all. "Dad!" he said into the phone.

"Hi, Mark. What did your mother say about me when she told you I was on the phone?"

"Nothing, she just said you were on the phone. I'm doing really well in school."

"Nothing? I thought she said, 'Your father is *actually* on the phone.'"

"No, Dad. I got a hundred on a math test this week."

"Be sure to tell your mother that she has no right to comment on how often I talk to you and your sister because *she's* the one who won't let me come visit."

Mark tightened his lips. He didn't know if that was true or not. "Dad, I got a hundred on a math test this week. And I got an A on an English essay." He didn't mention that the essay was just about what he did over the summer.

"Not an A-plus?"

"No," Mark said, silently cursing Mrs. Quigley. "My teacher doesn't *give* A-pluses."

"What kind of an idiot doesn't give A-pluses?" his dad said. "Have you entered the Mastermind tournament? You know I won that every year in junior high."

Mark knew. He had spent hours looking at the trophies with his dad's name on them in the family room, before his dad left and took the trophies with him. "I haven't heard anything about it yet," Mark said. "But don't worry. I've got it made. Dad, guess what? There's this other kid named Mark Geoffrey Hopper—"

Mark's mother shouted that dinner was ready.

"I'm on the phone!" Mark shouted back.

"Then get off of it. It's dinnertime."

"What was that? What's your mother on about now?" his dad asked.

"Nothing," Mark said bitterly.

"Let me talk to your sister."

"But we just started talking," Mark said quietly.

"What was that?"

"Nothing. Hold on." He started to feel funny, like he was going to cry. Rather than give in to it and get made fun of by Beth and his mother, he gave his dad his I-don't-like-you-either look through the phone. He wasn't sure if he was glad or not that his dad couldn't see it. He put the phone down and walked into the kitchen, where Beth and his mom were starting to eat pork chops. "You're eating without me?" he asked.

Beth shrugged. "You were on the phone," she said with her mouth full.

Their mom slapped Beth's hand. "You're fourteen years old. Close your mouth when you eat."

"Do you want to talk to Dad?" Mark asked her.

"No," said Beth. She kept cutting a pork chop with vigor, then made a show of taking the piece off her fork with her teeth.

"He wants to talk to you," Mark said.

"Well, I don't want to talk to him," Beth said. She stuck out her tongue, which was covered in pork-chop mush. Some of the mush dripped out of her mouth and onto her plate.

"I'll talk to him," their mother said with a sigh. She got up from the table and wiped her hands.

Mark ran back to the phone. "Mom's coming," he said. "Bye, Dad!" He handed the phone to his mother hesitantly. This could be good or bad. From the way he heard his mom say his dad's name, he knew it was bad. He stomped back into the kitchen, plopped down into a chair, stabbed his fork into a pork chop, and ate. He needed more evidence of artistic or athletic talent. He was more determined than ever to win the Mastermind tournament; that would make his dad realize how much he liked and missed his son. And when he had a trophy that matched his dad's three, they'd need to place them all right next to one another, which meant his dad would *have* to come back.

Chapter 3

Mark Proves Himself Useless

"Can I practice something on you, Grandpa?" Mark asked Grandpa Murray that night after dinner.

"Sure." Grandpa Murray put down his half-finished crossword puzzle and assumed a boxer's stance.

Mark laughed. "It's not something like that," he said.

"It's not for that turkey who stole your name?"

"Well, sort of. My math teacher, Miss Payley, said she thinks I should have a study partner, which would be fine. But the study partner she gave me is the other Mark Hopper."

"Good grief."

"So I am going to go to Miss Payley tomorrow after class and tell her"—he took a deep breath—"that I really like the idea of having a study partner, but I'd like it if it was someone else."

"Okay," said Grandpa Murray. "So what do you want to practice on me?"

"That was it."

"What was it?"

"What I just said. I really like the idea of having a study partner, but I'd like it if it was someone else."

"Okay," said Grandpa Murray. "So what are you going to do about it?"

"Talk to Miss Payley tomorrow!" Mark said, laughing.

"And what are you going to say? Go ahead and practice it on me."

Mark laughed so hard that he fell over. "I said it already!" he said.

"You did? How did I miss it? Say it again. After the part about wanting your study partner to be someone else."

Mark's stomach hurt from laughing so hard. He wasn't worried about talking to Miss Payley anymore. He thanked Grandpa Murray for his help through his puffs of laughter and left the room. Grandpa Murray, still confused, called after him, "What's so funny? I mean it, practice what you want to say on me!"

Mark walked back to the room holding his stomach. "Forget it, Grandpa," he said. "Just wish me luck for tomorrow."

Grandpa Murray shrugged and shook Mark's hand. "Good luck, kid."

Mark tried hard to pay attention in math the next day, but he was so worried about talking to Miss Payley after class that everything else seemed to drift through his head without even pausing in his brain, let alone finding a home there. The other

Mark seemed to never put down his hand, as usual, and Mark thought that if he weren't such a jerk, he probably would be a useful person to study with. Sometimes he caught himself thinking about his appeal to Miss Payley instead of his simplifying-fractions practice problems, and then his mind drifted to how he needed to go over this stuff with a study partner later, since he wasn't taking in any of it now. Then he'd pray that that partner wouldn't be Mark Hopper, and the cycle would continue.

When class ended, Mark told Jonathan to save him a seat in the cafeteria and dawdled at his desk, waiting for everyone to leave so he could talk to Miss Payley in private. But one person was also dawdling, and that was the other Mark Hopper. Mark's eyes widened at his bad luck.

"Aren't you going to lunch now?" Mark hissed at Mark.

"I wanted to speak to Miss Payley about something first," Mark replied quietly.

"Well, hurry up, then," Mark said. "I'm waiting to speak to her, too." He was clutching a piece of loose-leaf paper: his lists.

"You can go first," Mark offered.

Mark didn't want Mark there when he gave his lists to Miss Payley, but he could not pass up a chance to be first at anything, so he said, "Suit yourself. Miss Payley, may I please speak with you for a minute?"

Miss Payley looked up and smiled. "Sorry, Mark. And Mark. I don't have time to talk to you boys right now."

"But this will be quick," Mark protested.

Miss Payley shook her head and said she'd speak to them after school when they arrived for their study session, before rushing out the door.

One Mark sighed and the other growled a bit. Neither

wanted to wait until after school because that meant being there with the other after school; being there together right now was bad enough. But neither had a choice.

After school, Miss Payley waited until both Marks had arrived to say she was ready to listen.

The Mark with the list presented it to her. "I wanted to tell you that even though I really want Mark to do well in math, I just don't have time to be Mark's study partner. Here, I made a list of reasons. And of some other possible solutions to the problem."

The other Mark felt his eyes widen at his luck. "I understand!" he volunteered. "I am fine with having a different study partner."

The first Mark looked at him with a crooked grin. He couldn't believe they had something in common.

Miss Payley skimmed Mark's list and handed it back. "I appreciate your point of view," she said, "but as I said yesterday, I think you two will work wonderfully together. And that's that."

"But—"

"Mark—"

"But really, I—"

"Mark. Thank you both for showing up. I am going to do some of my work in the teachers' lounge down the hall, but I will be back to check on you. There is nothing to frown about, Mark—or to bare your teeth at me for, Mark. You two sit down and work on simplifying fractions—together. Or you will both receive a zero for class participation."

One Mark's shoulders sank in disappointment while the other's flew up in rage. But Miss Payley walked out of the room, leaving them with no one to turn to but each other.

"This is so unfair," Mark growled.

"I know," Mark agreed.

"I don't know why Miss Payley even thinks I can help you. You're hopeless."

"I don't think that's true," Mark whispered. "I'm just having a hard time adjusting."

Mark let out a snide laugh. "Yeah. Okay."

The two boys stared at each other with pure disdain. Finally, Mark sighed and sat down and took out his binder. He wanted to start the math homework, but he quickly realized that he had didn't really have any clue as to how to simplify fractions. He stared at the first problem with his eyes shaped like large zeroes.

"What are you doing?" Mark demanded.

"The homework," Mark said. "Since we have to be here anyway."

"But you're just staring at it."

"I'm taking my time."

"Oh, boy, you really are dumb," Mark said. He was looking over Mark's shoulder. "The first one is so easy a two-day-old baby could do it."

"Then how do you do it?" Mark said earnestly. He thought maybe he could trick the other Mark into being of some help.

"You just—" Mark started. Then he stopped himself and crossed his arms. "Look it up," he said.

Miss Payley poked her head in the doorway and saw Mark sitting with his homework out and the other Mark over his shoulder. "Looking good, boys," she said before leaving again.

Mark stared at his blank homework. He started to doodle

in the corner of the page. "And you think you're good at every-thing," he said under his breath.

"What was that?" fired Mark.

Mark took a deep breath. "You think you're good at every-thing, but you're not very good at helping people," he said. He continued to draw. The sketch was of a cartoon figure staring at a piece of paper with numbers and question marks floating around his head.

Mark watched the figure take shape on Mark's page. His face grew red. "I am *great* at helping people. I am the best helper in the whole world. I just don't want to help you."

"Why not?" Mark asked.

Mark was taken aback. "Because," he said. "You're hope-less. You're ruining the name Mark Geoffrey Hopper."

"*I'm* ruining it?" Mark said, his eyes wide. He laughed a little. "Sorry," he said, covering his mouth. But he couldn't help it. He laughed some more.

"What are you laughing about?"

Mark tried to answer. And to stop laughing. But he couldn't. He sketched another figure on his paper. It had a large scowl and pointy, down-turned eyebrows. Since he was laughing so hard that his body was shaking, the figure's hair came out squig-gly and unkempt.

Mark wanted to tear up Mark's paper. He did not look like that—his hair was neatly gelled! He also wanted to tear it up be-cause it wasn't fair that Mark could draw something that good in such a short amount of time.

Miss Payley peeked back in. Her eyebrows were raised. "Looks like you are having a fun time," she said.

Both Marks snorted, though only one meant to.

"You are free to go whenever you're ready," Miss Payley continued. "But how about you have a second session on Wednesday at the same time? That way you two can prepare for Thursday's quiz together." Neither responded, and Miss Payley said, "Yes? Perfect!"

After Miss Payley left again, Mark finally stopped laughing. He put down his pencil. "Do you want to help me with tonight's homework?" he asked. "I really don't know how to simplify fractions."

The other Mark sneered. "Yeah. Because I really want to help someone who laughed at me for ten minutes and drew a mean picture of me."

"But we don't have a choice," Mark said, not denying that the drawing was of Mark. "Why don't we just make the best of it?"

Mark actually considered it for a moment. But why should he give away all of his knowledge, especially to someone who was too shy to even speak to a teacher? He did all of his homework without any help; why should the other Mark Hopper have an unfair advantage? He already had an unfair advantage when it came to art. He watched Mark finish up his little sketch and sign his initials at the bottom of it—*MGH* in loopy, childlike script. Mark's brain switched into overdrive. Thinking at ten miles a minute and only pausing to give the other Mark a what-a-pity-you're-hopeless-at-math look, Mark put on his backpack, tightened the straps, and stomped out the door.

Chapter 14

Mark Proves Himself Useful

"Hey, neighbor." Jasmina tapped Mark on the shoulder at his locker.

"What?" said Mark. He continued to organize his PRIVATE AND NONE OF YOUR BUSINESS binders on his locker shelves. It would have weakened the effect of his storming out of school last week if he had stopped to organize his locker, so he still had some morning binders on the afternoon shelves. Since he prided himself on neatness (and got a blue ribbon for most organized desk in third grade), he couldn't stand it.

"I'll wait," said Jasmina. She chewed on the tip of one of her braids.

Mark sorted his binders more slowly.

"Oh, come on," she said. "I want to talk to you. Can't you just look up or something?"

"It is rude to rush someone."

"You're one to talk about being rude," Jasmina scoffed. "That's what I want to talk to you about. The other Mark told me you refused to help him with math. What is wrong with you?"

"What do you mean?" Mark asked innocently. All of his books were on their proper shelves, but he didn't stand up or turn around.

"He's a nice guy," Jasmina said. "Everybody likes him. And he's a *really* good artist. What do you have against him?"

"If you think he's so nice and talented, why don't *you* teach him math?"

"I would," Jasmina said, "but Miss Payley won't let me. I asked."

Mark stayed down so Jasmina wouldn't see how taken aback he was. Jasmina was *his* friend, and even though he hated him, Mark was *his* problem. "What, do you *like* him?" he sang. "Oooh."

"I like him a lot more than I like you right now," Jasmina countered.

Mark stood up and whirled around. "You can't possibly. We've been friends since preschool," he said. "He just moved in. You don't even know him."

"Neither do you," Jasmina said. She crossed her arms. Having been friends with Mark since preschool, she knew two things about winning an argument with him: (1) Don't bother trying, but (2) If you do bother trying, make him think he's won. She decided to go for the second one. "Look," she said. "You're really smart, and a really good person, so he clearly looks up to you," she lied.

Mark puffed out his chest a bit. "Duh," he said.

Jasmina hit him with her backpack. "So—you probably already know this—but the smart thing to do is help him out."

"I did know that already," Mark said with a sneer. As he said it, however, he realized that it was true.

"I figured," said Jasmina. "So just be nice. You may even get something out of it."

Mark knew that Jasmina probably meant he'd find that being nice would get him far—he'd heard *that* enough in school assemblies—or that he'd actually start to like the other Mark. But he thought about it in other, more important terms: the Mastermind tournament and evidence of artistic talent. He had a plan, and it would be a lot harder to accomplish if he and Mark Hopper were archenemies. "All right," he said to Jasmina. "But only because I'm a good person."

Jasmina nodded solemnly before breaking into a grin. She wanted to pat herself on the back, but in keeping with the second rule for arguing with Mark Hopper, she threw her arms around him and squeezed tightly instead.

Mark the Team Player

Mark Geoffrey Hopper had been confused when he'd discovered that his new town already had a Mark Geoffrey Hopper, but he was even more confused when that Mark Geoffrey Hopper became friendly—or tried to, at least. In homeroom, Mark turned around to face him and asked how he was finding it in Greenburgh so far. And when Mark, assuming Mark was asking in order to tell him to move away, replied cautiously that it was fine, the other Mark just gave an even bigger forced smile and said, "Well, let me know if you want me to show you around or something sometime." The new Mark's mouth dropped open into an *O*, matching the shape of his eyes. He was too shocked to even say thank you. He thought he might be dreaming, until the other Mark added, "I pretty much know everything about the town." Mark thought that was a little more like Mark, but he pinched a piece of his arm just to make sure.

In social studies that morning, Mark read (quietly) out loud his report about ancient Egyptian superstitions. When Mr. Rocco asked if there were any questions or comments, the other Mark raised his hand. The presenting Mark braced himself for the worst—the other Mark had pointed out mistakes or asked impossible questions to every other presenter so far. But this time Mark simply said, "I thought that was really interesting."

Even Mr. Rocco's eyes widened in response. "Really?" said Mr. Rocco. "I mean," he said, remembering that he was the teacher, "did you find any part of it particularly interesting?"

Mark said, "Yes. I didn't know that Egyptians worshipped cats."

"Thank you," said Mr. Rocco. "Yes, that was a very interesting part."

The presenting Mark was still too shocked at the other Mark's comments to be proud of himself.

The other Mark raised his hand once more. "Actually," he said quickly when Mr. Rocco called on him again, "I *did* already know that, but it was still interesting." He sneer-smiled at Mark, but Mark thought it actually looked slightly more like a smile than a sneer. Convinced Mark was being nice because he had already done something mean, he checked his chair thoroughly for anything pointy, sticky, or Scotch-taped, but it seemed clear. (Actually, he didn't get a chance to check it as thoroughly as he wanted to because Mr. Rocco said, "Is something wrong with your chair, Mark?" and he had to say no and sit down quickly.)

"Mark Hopper is being really, really nice," Mark whispered to Jonathan in the locker room before gym.

"Serious?" said Jonathan, glancing around for the other Mark, whose gym locker was one aisle over.

"Yeah," Mark whispered. "It's really weird."

"That's scary," Jonathan said. "Maybe you're going to get home and find that he killed your cat or something."

"I don't have a cat."

"Maybe he got you a cat and then killed it."

Mark stood far away from the other Mark while the gym teacher led the class through the presport stretches. But after stretching, Mark came next to him and said, "You're really good at that hamstring stretch."

Jonathan, who was still standing on one foot and stretching the other leg, fell over.

"Um, thanks," Mark said.

"A lot of people don't realize that stretching is really important," Mark continued. "But you're pretty good at it. Like me."

The gym teacher selected two boys to be captains for a soccer game, and they stepped in front of the group to choose their players. Kenny Yolent took Jonathan and Paul Grotosky, and Pete Dale chose Tyrell Smith and Cole Zitoff. Then Pete pointed to Mark Hopper, who was standing next to Mark Hopper. "I'll take Hopper," he said.

Both Marks stepped forward. They stopped and looked at each other.

"I'm really good at soccer," said the Mark who had been acting strangely friendly.

Pete rolled his eyes and pointed to the other Mark. "I want *that* Hopper."

"Are you sure?" asked Mark in a way that suggested Pete was choosing creamed spinach over chocolate cake.

"It's okay," said the other Mark. "You go be on Pete's team."

"What?" said Pete. "I'm the captain. I pick *you* Hopper, not *you* Hopper." He turned to the second one. "Get over yourself," he said.

Mark glared at Pete and said, "Your team's loss, diaper breath." Then he patted the other Mark on the back and said, through his teeth, "No offense."

Mark walked to stand by Pete and Jonathan with his eyes as round as soccer balls. A few rounds of picking later, no one was left but the other Mark Hopper and Jim Sewell, who, no matter what the sport, picked up the ball and threw it. Kenny picked Jim, and Pete had no choice but to take the other Mark after all.

The Mark chosen last usually tried to score every time he got the ball, no matter how far he was from the goal. But when the ball came to him at the very end of the class period, he passed it to the other Mark, who kicked it to score the winning goal. The whole team cheered and patted Mark on the back, including the other Mark, who patted so hard he almost knocked Mark over.

The Mark who scored, still concerned that Mark's friendliness was all a front, decided to fight fire with fire—or, in this case, roses with roses. He took Mark's hand in his, shook it tightly, and then raised it in the air. "That was a great assist!" he shouted.

The other teammates looked at one another. Then Jonathan stepped up and patted both Marks on the back. "Awesome pass!" he yelled. "All right, team!"

Tyrell and Cole followed. They jumped on Mark's back and hollered. Even Pete Dale shook Mark's hand. The gym teacher blew his whistle, and all of the boys ran back to the locker room chanting "Mark and Mark! Mark and Mark!"

Chapter **16δ**

Mark's Talent

Being friendly was exhausting. After a whole day of being nice to Mark Hopper, Mark left school straight after eighth period. He wanted to just walk home alone and collapse on his bed for a little while, but Jasmina caught up with him and started talking. She talked about Kylie's new haircut ("Don't you think it's cute?") and Becky's skirt ("I thought Becky had better fashion sense than to wear something with leopard print!") and that day's school lunch ("The soup was pretty good but, really, who would want pot roast for lunch—especially when it looks green?"), and Mark didn't have the energy to say that he didn't care about Kylie's haircut and he cared even less about Becky's skirt. He didn't even bother pointing out that if she was half as smart as him, she would bring lunch instead of eating the cafeteria food. He also didn't tell Jasmina about his assist in the soccer game. He just kept quiet. Yet when they arrived at their houses, Jasmina gave Mark a big hug for the second time that day and told him that he really was a good friend. "Want to come over?" she asked. "You can help Timmy with his homework."

Mark didn't ask what kind of homework a first grader gets and what kind of dummy would need help with it; he just shook his head.

"Okay, we do have a lot of homework," Jasmina said. "Do you want to play running bases later?"

Mark shrugged.

Jasmina shrugged, too. "Talk to you later!"

Mark went inside and sank into the couch, backpack, bassoon, and all. He rubbed his cheeks—they hurt from all of his forced smiling—and sat staring at the blank television. All day he'd been reminding himself silently of how making the other Mark like and trust him was the key part of his plan for the Mastermind tournament—*artistic talent, artistic talent*—and it gave him the drive to continue. He was trying so hard to be nice to the other Mark Hopper, yet Mark just kept looking at him with that same deer-in-headlights look. It was so frustrating. Mark thought about how he would have to help the other Mark Hopper with math after school on Wednesday and of all the long days in between during which he'd have to—*ugh*—keep making himself smile. But then he started thinking about that afternoon's soccer game and his success—well, *their* success—and how it wasn't really *that* bad that he had to share it. He felt his mouth turn into a smile all by itself.

The next few days, Mark Hopper found being nice to Mark Hopper to be less tiring. It was less of an effort to talk to him, and his cheeks stopped hurting in the afternoon. It wasn't that he *liked* the other Mark, he insisted to himself. He simply was getting better at pretending to like him. He told himself that being nice to the other Mark Hopper was like a test, and he had never failed a test—ever—so he wasn't about to start now. He especially wasn't going to fail at something because of the other Mark. So by Wednesday, he wasn't *looking forward* to helping Mark with math, but he wasn't dreading it, either.

When they did meet and review for the test, Mark was very attentive and respectful of Mark's fractions expertise. He listened to what Mark had to say and improved his skills throughout the half hour. It still took Mark longer to do one problem than it took Mark to do five problems, but Mark tried not to be too impatient or smug about it. Every time he wanted to say something like "Boy you're slow!" or "You're only on question three? I've already finished the whole page!" he said something like "What type of things do you usually draw?" or "Do you usually write out your whole name when you sign your drawings?" instead.

And after the test the next day, he didn't ask Miss Payley if he could leave class early since he finished first. Instead, he waited until the period was over and went up to Mark as the class filed out into the hall. "How'd the test go?" he asked, truly interested.

"I don't want to jinx it," Mark said, "but not bad! I think our study session really helped."

"I'm glad you thought our study session really helped!" Mark repeated loudly in Miss Payley's direction. He continued asking Mark questions about different parts of the test all the way down to the cafeteria, where he sat at Mark and Jonathan's table. Mark pretended to be interested in Mark and Jonathan's conversation about the art club, but he really didn't care about what they had to say. The teacher was going to choose some of their paintings to put up in the local library—big deal. Jonathan asked Mark how his portrait was coming along, and the Mark who thought art was for wimps said with over-the-top interest, "Oh, you're making a portrait?"

"Yeah," Mark answered. "It's coming along okay."

"Okay?" Jonathan looked past the Mark next to him to talk to the other. "His is *really* good," he said. "I mean, *really* good."

One Mark's ears turned red. The other Mark stuffed some sandwich into his mouth to keep himself from saying something unfriendly.

Jonathan looked back at the Mark who was his friend. "Are you still working on his body? Or did you start adding other things?"

"I finished a rough sketch of the body," Mark said. "But I still need to work on it. I'm glad it's not due for a while."

"Yeah," agreed Jonathan. "I still don't even know who I'm going to do my portrait of. But I narrowed it down to either my godmother or Superman."

One Mark laughed. The other could not help but make his that's-the-dumbest-thing-I've-ever-heard look, but he was trying to be nice, so he did it facing the other way and into his hand.

"I'm doing my grandpa," Mark told Mark. "We're only in the sketching stage now. Later we have to paint it, and it's our main grade for this marking period. But if it's picked to go to the library, we won't get it back until later, because they don't know when the library show is going to be yet." He reached into his backpack and pulled out a sketchbook. He flipped to the page with the drawing of an old man that Mark had seen him showing Jonathan the week before, though it was now a lot more developed. "My grandpa Murray," Mark told Mark.

The picture was very detailed, and Mark couldn't help but take a small gasp at its beauty. (He tried to pass the gasp off as the beginning of a cough, and said that a bite of his turkey sandwich had gone down the wrong pipe.) The man, Grandpa Murray, was sitting on a sofa. He was wearing a V-neck undershirt tucked into a pair of worn trousers. His wispy hairs were going every which way, and a small smile, as though he was pleasantly surprised to see something up ahead, was on his lightly wrinkled face. A half-eaten apple was in one of his hands and a folded newspaper was on his lap. Even though it was only a rough sketch, the apple looked so real it looked like it would brown if left half eaten. There was no doubt that this drawing was evidence of artistic talent.

"He really has more wrinkles," Mark said. "But I'm going to leave them out."

"Yeah, my godmother has really big teeth. So if I end up doing her, I'll probably make them smaller."

"What if you do Superman?" Mark asked as he put away the sketchbook.

"Then I'll make his muscles extra big, so if I ever get to show it to him, he'll like it."

"Maybe you can make your godmother's muscles extra big, too, if you end up painting her," Mark said.

"And make her wearing a Superman outfit!" Jonathan added. "The best of both!"

"It's a bird, it's a plane, no, it's . . ." the other Mark chimed in.

"Super Godmother!" said Jonathan.

"Godmotherman!" said Mark at the same time.

Through his laughter, Mark wondered if the other Mark would finish his portrait in time for his plan to work. But then he decided not to think about the plan. "The godmother of steel!" he said.

"Just call on Godmotherman!" Jonathan continued in the tone of a television announcer. "Her perfume is so strong it will send the bad guys running!"

"Or at least they'll have to stop hurting you to hold their nose!"

"Beware, bad guys! Her big teeth will reflect the light into your eyes and blind you!"

"And then while you're blinded, she'll whack you with her pocketbook!"

"And when she goes into the phone booth to change back into a regular godmother, she'll make a call and never come out."

Chapter 17

The Trouble with the Rules

"Rise and shine, Mark-fart!"

Mark gasped and sat straight up. Someone only woke him up if he overslept. He looked at his clock: 6:15 A.M. He didn't need to get up for a half hour. "What's going on?" he asked as he focused his eyes.

"It's time to get up," Beth said.

"Not for me."

"It's not?"

"No."

Beth slapped her forehead. "Oh, whoops! I was thinking you had school at the same time as me." She started out sincere, but by the end she couldn't help but smirk.

Mark's eyes narrowed. "You knew I didn't have to get up and did it on purpose!" he shouted.

Beth shrugged, her mouth in a tight sneer. Mark hurled his pillow at her. Beth screamed. "Mom! Mark threw a pillow at me!"

"She deserves it!" Mark screamed. "She woke me up just to be mean!"

"Knock it off!" their mother screamed back.

Mark searched for something else to throw. He contemplated his lamp but settled for the heaviest book on his nightstand. He held it above his head with both hands. Beth screeched and ran into the hallway as he let go. The book hit the door frame and slid down.

Beth peeked her head in and chirped, "I'm off to school! Sorry to wake you up too early! Have a *great* day, baby brother!"

Mark hurled his second-heaviest book at her, and Beth ducked. "Now, now," she said like a teacher, waving her finger at him. "No need to get upset, Marky."

Mark was seething with anger. Beth stuck out her tongue at him and left, whistling.

Mark looked at his clock again: 6:17. He was too worked up to go back to sleep. And anyway, his pillow was in the hallway. He threw both legs out from under the covers and stomped into the hall. His books were sprawled open and down on the floor, the pages crinkled and torn. He picked them up so harshly that they closed with the pages folded, which only made him angrier, so he threw them across the room.

"What is going on up there?" shouted Mark's mother.

"Nothing!" Mark shouted back. But he heard his mother stomping up the stairs. He picked up his books and smoothed them out before placing them back on his nightstand.

"What happened?" his mother asked. It wasn't even six-thirty in the morning and she looked worn out from her day.

"Your *daughter*," Mark said, "woke me up a half hour early just to be mean." He thought he saw his mom trying not to smile. "It's not funny," he hissed. "Why did you have to have her? You should have just gone straight to having me."

"Now come on," she said. "Beth makes things more interesting around here."

"Interesting in a bad way."

"So you're getting an early start on the day. Make the most of it. Practice your bassoon or something."

"I already know all of the songs for the winter concert, and it's only October. They're all baby songs. I could have played them in second grade."

"You didn't learn to play the bassoon until third grade."

"Exactly."

"You have such an ear for music. You'd think in eleven years we could find something you weren't good at."

Mark puffed out his chest. "My soccer team won in gym class the other day. And everyone chanted my name on the way to the locker room."

"You told me. You're our little prodigy. I'm sure you'll find some way to make use of this extra half hour."

"It's actually only twenty minutes now, I guess."

Mrs. Hopper checked her watch. "Oh, cripes. You're going to make me late for work." She gave Mark a frustrated look and hurried out of his room. "And get your pillow out of my hallway!" she shouted. "Don't be such a slob!"

After that short talk with his mother, Mark grumbled, stomped, and thrashed through his morning routine. He scrubbed himself so roughly in the shower that he turned his skin red. He brushed his teeth so violently that he bent the toothbrush bristles. Then he gelled his hair so forcefully that it came out looking and feeling like a helmet. He did not know how he was going to be friendly to Mark today, and today mattered extra because it was a Wednesday.

Mark left for school early, not waiting for Jasmina or even going by her house. While he sorted his books at his locker, Frank Stucco passed by and closed the locker door on him, making Mark whirl around and call, "Why are you here so early, Frank? Morning detention?" He then used some of his extra time to figure out which homeroom was Frank's and tell his homeroom teacher on him. The other Mark said "good morning" to him in Mrs. Frances's room, with his usual dumb, half-frightened stare and goofy half smile, and Mark couldn't help but bark, "Maybe for you."

In social studies, Mark was leaning far back in his chair, not even bothering to sit up straight when he raised his hand to answer every question (or to grumble when Mr. Rocco didn't call on him), when Mr. Rocco said something that made him perk up instantly. "What I am about to pass around now," Mr. Rocco said, "is information and application forms for this year's Mastermind tournament."

Mark shot his hand straight into the air. "When is the tournament this year? And when is everything due?" he asked.

"I believe the tournament's in December, and everything's due in November," Mr. Rocco said impatiently.

"November what?" He wanted to know exactly how much time he had to prepare, and how many more weeks he had of being friendly to Mark Hopper before putting his plan into action. With a rough estimate of six weeks until Thanksgiving, he figured it was still too early to start the plan that afternoon at his and Mark's study session.

"I'm not sure, Mark. All of the information is in the packet I am about to distribute." He took a pile of papers from his desk into his arms. "The Mastermind tournament—"

Mark raised his hand again. "Do you still need report cards, an essay, a public speech, an interview, and evidence of artistic and-slash-or athletic talent?"

The class snickered and whispered. Mr. Rocco raised his eyebrows. "Yes, Mark, that's mostly right. I'm glad you're so interested in the tournament. If you'll please let me speak for a few minutes, some other students who might be interested can learn about it, too."

He continued to give the class an overview of the tournament and its requirements, but Mark was stuck on the words *mostly right.* What was *mostly* right about what he'd said? He had studied the tournament rules through and through. He had dreamed about them more than one night. Could the rules have changed? Maybe Mr. Rocco was just saying Mark was only *mostly* right so as not to appear as though he knew less than one of his students. But what if the rules had changed? Maybe they now only wanted one piece of evidence of artistic talent! Mark raised his hand. "Mr. Rocco," he said without waiting to be called on, "have the rules changed since last year?"

Mr. Rocco sighed. "Yes, Mark, as I was saying, there is a new element of the competition this year in place of the public speech. The committee thought that the tournament did not emphasize teamwork and collaboration as much as they'd like, and so this year, they are going to have the entrants work as a team during the final round. These pamphlets will give you more details, but the idea is that the winner should be not only a strong individual, but someone others enjoy working with."

A short, stocky boy who sat in the back of the room raised his hand. "When you say a strong individual, do you mean like someone who can rip a phone book in half with his bare hands?"

Mark didn't sneer or comment or even give Mr. Rocco his what's-wrong-with-kids-these-days look. He was stuck on the new rules. The Mastermind tournament was about being the best. That meant competing with the other contestants, not working with them as a team. How could they change the rules to something that involved collaboration? That meant changing the whole point of the tournament. And more importantly, how could they change the rules on *him*? This day could not get any worse.

"Yes, Mark?"

"I didn't say anything," Mark snapped, wondering if he had been thinking aloud.

"That's why I called on the other Mark," said Mr. Rocco. "Go ahead, Mark."

"Can anybody enter?"

"Yes, anyone in middle school can enter. There are no requirements about age or grades or activities. It's open to all. And I encourage you all to give it a try."

"Is there a cash prize?" asked the boy who wanted to rip a phone book in half with his bare hands.

"No, no cash, unfortunately. But there's a big trophy. And lots of bragging rights. This tournament has been around for almost one hundred and fifty years, and it is very prestigious. You can read about the history of the tournament when I pass around the information."

Mr. Rocco passed around the pamphlets just as the bell rang. Mark put the pamphlet in his folder and went up to Mr. Rocco's desk. "Mr. Rocco," he said, "why did they change the rules?"

Mr. Rocco talked while he straightened up his desk. "I told you, Mark. They wanted the competition to include more team-work."

"But the contest is about one person winning. One person."

"Are you thinking of entering?" Mr. Rocco asked casually.

"Thinking?" Mark scoffed. "I've been preparing for over a year now. And I've been planning for longer than that. My dad won the Mastermind tournament every year he was in middle school. We have the trophies in my house to prove it." He didn't care that this was a lie; it was none of Mr. Rocco's business that his dad had left and so had the trophies.

"That's great," Mr. Rocco said. "Good luck."

"But don't you see the problem?" Mark asked. "I have been preparing with the old rules. Now all my hard work was for nothing"—he threw his hands in the air—"and it's not fair! Why would they change the rules anyway?"

Mr. Rocco looked at Mark and sighed. "I am not on the tournament committee, Mark."

"How can I contact someone who is?"

Mr. Rocco tried not to smile. "Well, there must be some contact information on the pamphlet I handed out. But I think it's a little late for them to change the rules for this year."

Mark tightened his mouth. He didn't say it, but he knew Mr. Rocco was probably right.

"Think of it this way, Mark," Mr. Rocco tried. "Everyone has the same rules, and no one knows what to expect from these new ones. So everyone who enters is in the same boat. And if anyone else had been preparing like you had—they'd probably be your primary competition, right?—they are in your exact situation right now. Besides, a little teamwork never hurt anybody."

"It's not that I'm not good at it," Mark said quickly. He thought of the soccer game in gym and his conversation with Mark and Jonathan at lunch the day before and wondered if he really was good at teamwork. "It's that it's not fair."

"Well, at least look over the new rules before you contact the committee. That's my free good-sport tip of the day."

Mark turned to leave.

"And Mark," Mr. Rocco called after him, "when someone answers a question or gives you some advice, it's nice to say thank you or at least good-bye before you leave."

"Good-bye," Mark mumbled. Thanks for nothing, he thought.

Mark's Strength, Mark's Weakness

"What are you looking at?" Mark asked, his wide eyes peering over Mark's backpack to see.

"None of your beeswax," Mark snapped. "Just do some problems on your own or something for a few minutes."

Mark shrugged and turned to the math. He had paid very close attention that day when Miss Payley went over how to convert mixed numbers into improper fractions, but of course now that he was looking at a page of problems, he had no idea what to do. It had something to do with adding and multiplying . . . or was it subtracting and dividing? "So you . . . add and then divide?" he asked the other Mark cautiously.

"What? Look it up," Mark said. He glared harder at the Mastermind pamphlet, as though he could intimidate it into changing its content. "I'm busy."

Mark frowned. "Are you having a bad day?" he asked.

Mark softened a bit. No one had ever really asked him how his day was going before. "I just don't have time for this. It was going to be bad enough preparing for the Mastermind tournament without them changing the rules."

"Oh! That's the thing Mr. Rocco was talking about, right? What is it all about?"

"What is it *about*? It's about being the best." In one long, impassioned rant, Mark explained the history of the tournament and the fact that his father had won it three years in a row. He told Mark how long he'd been preparing, how *moronic* it was that they changed the rules (though he was sure to win anyway), and how big a trophy the winner got. He told him everything except the part about having more than one artistic ability.

"Wow. That sounds really hard."

"Oh, it takes a lot of planning, but it's not *hard*."

Mark doodled a trophy on a piece of loose-leaf paper. Then, with just a few tiny strokes of his pencil, he made it look as though the trophy was glistening in the sun. "Maybe I'll enter it," he said. How impressed his family would be if he won something like that for being smart! It would be like the day he found out he was in all honors classes, only ten times more exciting.

"Ha," Mark said with his you-couldn't-beat-me-if-you-tried look. "I mean," he added, "you *could*. But it's really a *lot* of work. So if you don't think you could win in every single part—the *good grades* and the *essay* and everything—it's really not worth it." He had to make sure there weren't any other report cards or essays with the name Mark Hopper on them. And that there wasn't another drawing with that name, either.

"Yeah, I guess," Mark said. His face twisted into a half frown.

"But that new teamwork part sounds fun. I like when you have to do something as a group. Like in gym when you have to hold hands with a big group and tangle yourselves up and then find a way out of it. We did that at my old school."

"Whatever," said Mark, not knowing what Mark was talking about and thinking that it didn't sound remotely fun. Holding hands in gym? Come on.

"You never did that?" Mark asked. He didn't say it, but he figured that was probably for the best. He couldn't picture Mark as much of a team player. He watched as Mark read the Mastermind rules as though they were his last chance of surviving all alone on a desert island. He was determined; he had to give him that. And when he stopped caring so much about being the best, he could even be kind of fun to talk to. It isn't that I *like* the other Mark, Mark thought, but some people might if he'd just give them a reason to. Mark thought all of this while absentmindedly sketching a miniature version of his portrait of Grandpa Murray. After a few minutes, he caught the other Mark studying *him* from the corner of his eye. "Sorry," he said, feeling his ears turn red. "I just really like drawing. I want to work on this drawing over the weekend, and my art teacher says we're allowed to take them home if we want, but it's just hard because my dad only comes to Greenburgh on weekends."

"Your dad doesn't live with you?" Mark asked, surprised.

Mark shook his head. "Not right now."

Mark eyed Mark curiously. He wanted to ask a lot of questions, but he didn't want Mark to ask any of him in return. He also kind of wanted to pat the other Mark on the back, but he didn't do that, either. What he did do was put the Mastermind rules aside and say, "We'd better do the math before Miss Payley comes in."

"You know," Mark said carefully after he had finished all of the math homework. "I can tell you about all of the team-work stuff we did at my old school. You know, the rules and things, and what the teachers were looking for when we did it. Maybe some of it will be the same at the tournament." He stole a quick glance at Mark's face—he didn't know if Mark would take his offer as a statement that he wasn't good enough to win the tournament on his own—and then went back to packing up his backpack. When he was finished packing up and the other Mark still hadn't said anything, Mark looked up to find him staring at him with his eyebrows raised.

"Why would you do that for me?" Mark asked.

Mark shrugged. "Why not? You're really helping me with the math. And I've done that sort of thing before, so that's some-thing I can help you with . . . maybe, if you want. Besides, since I'm not entering the tournament, I might as well help someone named Mark Hopper win." He chanced a smile.

Mark crossed his arms. "All right."

Mark widened his eyes in surprise. He nodded excitedly.

"Not that I couldn't do it on my own," Mark added quickly, "but it never hurts to be overprepared. And since we *have* to meet anyway . . . Maybe next week after we do the math we can start preparing?"

Mark kept nodding, like his head was on a spring. "Sure," he said. "I'll think about it and try to remember everything about it from last year. Cool! This'll be fun. See you later."

"Wait," Mark called. "Um, it's pretty stupid how you are so

scared to talk to teachers and stuff"—he wrinkled his forehead—
"I mean, you need to not be so scared to say what you think all
the time. Even argue sometimes . . . not necessarily as much as
me, but, you know . . ." He sighed. It was so hard to say what he
wanted to say when he was trying to be nice about it. "Anyway,
if you want, I can help you with that, too."

"All right," Mark said. "How about next Wednesday we talk
about that, too?"

"Okay."

"Okay."

They looked at each other awkwardly.

"All right."

"Okay. See you later."

"Oh, yeah. Have fun seeing your dad this weekend."

Mark laughed. "Thanks," he said. "But I'll see you tomorrow
in homeroom."

Chapter 19

Mark's Plan
Takes Shape

"Let's see . . ." Grandpa Murray rubbed his hands together and lifted his eyebrows a few times. He eyed the fruit aisle.

Mark mimicked Grandpa Murray's motion. "Yes, let's see . . ." he said before letting out a sinister laugh. When Grandpa Murray offered to do the grocery shopping, Mark had turned off the television, jumped up, and volunteered to go with him. He told his mom that he just wanted to help out, but really he wanted to go because Grandpa Murray was great to food-shop with. He'd put anything Mark asked for in the cart. In fact, he'd put anything at all in the cart as long as it looked tasty or interesting— beef jerky, sixteen-inch king crab legs, freeze-dried enchiladas, sugarcoated cheese curls covered in chocolate. One time he bought a box of cat food because the box boasted a large gold medal from *Cat Care* magazine, even though the Hoppers didn't have a cat. Mrs. Hopper must have suspected Mark's reason for wanting to go along—he never "wanted to help out" when *she* went to the supermarket—so she sent Beth along to keep the other two in line.

"Why don't we split up this list by category," Beth said, scanning the long list of mostly boring, healthy foods her mother had insisted they follow, "and meet up at the register with the shortest line in twenty minutes."

"Bah," said Grandpa Murray. "I'll never remember what I'm supposed to get or where to meet. But I guess if you don't want to"—Grandpa Murray let out a loud, fake sniffle—"spend time with your grandfather, who only wants to"—*sniff*—"love you, then that's"—*sniff*—"just fine."

Mark sniffed loudly. "I'll stay with you, Grandpa! Don't cry."

"What about you, Beth?" Grandpa Murray said with a large frown.

Beth looked around and rolled her eyes. "Yes, okay, we'll all stay together."

"Yippee!" Grandpa Murray said.

Beth looked around again. "You're embarrassing me," she whispered. "Let's just start shopping."

"Does this embarrass you?" Mark asked. He picked up a bunch of grapes and balanced it on his head while humming circus music.

"Yes, it does," Beth said. She grabbed the grapes, threw them in a plastic bag, and put them in the cart. "And now we have to buy those because they were on your head."

"Does this embarrass you?" Mark asked. He reached toward a pile of cantaloupes.

Beth moved to block him. "Whatever you were going to do,

yes, it does," she said. "And I don't want to have to buy canta-loupe."

"How about kiwis?" Grandpa Murray asked. He held up a couple of hairy brown fruits.

"Not on the list . . ." Beth said.

Grandpa Murray placed the kiwis in the cart. "List schmist," he said.

"How about this?" Mark asked. He held up a big, whole pineapple.

"I don't know how we're going to cut that," Grandpa Murray said, "but why not. I'm a sucker for fruit with spikes on it."

Beth laughed and put the list in her pocket. She picked up a two-pound mesh bag of strangely shaped objects that was la-beled IMPORTED. "Can we get this?" she asked.

Grandpa Murray said, "That's the spirit!" He signaled for her to put it in the cart.

They continued through the supermarket filling up the shop-ping cart with everything unusual or intriguing they passed, plus lettuce for Beth's earthworms and most of the items Leslie Hop-per had requested. Mark studied Grandpa Murray as he moved through the aisles picking up items and squinting sharply to examine them. He was almost ready to redraw his portrait of Grandpa Murray on canvas and begin painting. He wanted to make sure he got every detail right and that he captured the whole of his grandpa's character. It would be best to work on the portrait in the same room as his grandpa so that he could look at him as he went along, but he wanted the painting to be a surprise. Maybe even a birthday present.

"Grandpa?" Mark said as he placed a package of string cheese into the cart. "When is your birthday?"

"November thirty-second," Grandpa Murray said.

"Really?"

"I think so."

"Come on, Mark," Beth said. She bopped him on the head with a package of cheese cubes. "There is no November thirty-second. There's not even a November thirty-first."

Mark thought a moment. "Hey! No month has a thirty-second."

Grandpa Murray thought a moment. "No?" he said. "I guess that makes my birthday December second."

"Really?"

"Really."

Mark tried to hide his excitement by comparing wild cherry with exotic berry yogurt. December 2 was perfect timing. Even though the painting was due toward the end of October, he had just found out that the selected portraits would be displayed in the library starting on December 2! Then he would just have to figure out a way to get Grandpa Murray to go with him to library—he'd have to make something up, which might be kind of tricky, but he had time—and he could show him the portrait right on his birthday. What a present that would be!

"The gears in your head are spinning," Grandpa Murray said. "What are you planning on doing with that yogurt?"

Mark shrugged and placed a container of exotic berry yogurt in the cart. "Oh, nothing," he said. "I'm just thinking that I have a really, really good birthday present for you."

Grandpa Murray raised his eyebrows. "I do like yogurt," Grandpa Murray said, "but this might go bad by December."

Mark laughed and said that the gift wasn't yogurt, but he wouldn't give away any other clues. The three shoppers turned into the snacks aisle, and Mark's eyes became round at the sight of all of the cookies, cakes, and treats that Grandpa Murray would probably let them buy.

"You're Mark, right?"

Mark turned to see a girl his age. She had long blond hair in a long blond ponytail, and her T-shirt said IVY ROAD ROADRUNNERS with a picture of the school's mascot in the center. "Yeah," Mark said. "Is that shirt from Ivy Road Middle School?" he asked. Then he felt his ears turn red as he realized what a stupid question it was.

"Yep," said the girl. She started chewing on one of her fingernails. "You're in sixth grade, right? And you're friends with Jasmina, right?"

"Yeah," Mark said. At least he thought they were friends. He hoped this girl wouldn't ask Jasmina. Maybe she didn't really consider them friends. He had never been to her house after school or anything. At least he knew he was definitely in sixth grade . . . right?

"I'm Laurie," the girl said.

Mark tried to think of a question to ask her or anything to say that wouldn't sound stupid. Luckily, since the best he could come with was "So, you're food shopping," a woman toward the end of the aisle called Laurie over.

"That's my mom," Laurie said. "But maybe I'll see you around school. And," she continued, "my birthday's coming up, and I'm having a big party at my house. So what's your last name so I can give you an invitation?"

"Hopper," Mark said, his ears turning even redder.

"Mark Hopper. Got it." She smiled. "See you around!"

"Yeah." Mark turned to face Grandpa Murray and Beth, who

were both grinning. Beth tousled his hair, and Mark smoothed it back down.

"Oh, I'm sorry," Beth teased. "Does that embarrass you?"

"No," Mark lied.

"What if I talked about all of the earthworms we have at home *really* loudly? Would that embarrass you?"

"Beth," Mark warned.

"How about this, does this embarrass you?" Beth asked. She grabbed two long, thin packages of cookies and held them above her head like antlers.

"Grandpa!" Mark hissed. He glanced down the aisle to make sure Laurie and her mother had gone.

"Come on now, Beth," Grandpa Murray said. "Enough teasing your brother." He held out his hands.

"All right," Beth agreed, grinning. She gave Grandpa Murray the boxes of cookies and tousled Mark's hair again. "But really," she said, "I'm glad you're making friends. She seems really nice."

"Beth!" Mark said.

"What?" Beth laughed. "I just said she seems nice."

Grandpa Murray put the cookies on his own head like antlers. "Hello, Beth and Mark," he said in a robotic voice. "I have come from another planet."

Beth and Mark both scrambled to remove the boxes from their grandfather's head. They looked at each other and walked as far away from him as they could.

Chapter 20

Mark Knows,
Thank You

Mark was nervous. He wondered if Mark remembered what they were supposed to talk about once they finished the math.

Mark was nervous, too. He wondered if Mark remembered what they were supposed to talk about once they finished the math.

Mark slowly filled in the last answer on the math homework (423), and Mark slowly checked it (it was correct). Then they looked at each other.

"Thanks," said Mark.

"Yeah," said Mark.

"That's a good place to start," Mark said quietly.

"What?"

Mark spoke a little louder. "That's a good place to start preparing for the teamwork part of the Mastermind tournament."

"What is?" Mark asked. His lip was curled and his eyebrows pointed down.

"When someone says 'thanks,' you should just say 'you're welcome.' Instead of 'yeah' or something. At the tournament at least."

"I know," Mark said defensively.

"I know you do. So just don't forget to do it," he said earnestly. "And you probably know this, too, but when someone gives you a tip, like I just did, you could try saying 'thanks' instead of 'I know.'"

"I *know*. Geez."

"I know," said Mark. "But even if you do know, you should still say 'thank you,' because it makes them feel like you want to be on their team." He thought for a moment. "And I'm sure the judges will be looking for something like that when you do the teamwork thing. You'll probably get points for it."

"Whatever," Mark said. "They're pretty dumb if they're going to pick the winner based on a few 'thank yous' and 'you're welcomes.' That stuff doesn't even matter! What matters is that they ruined everything by changing the rules. Just watch—after they try it this new way a few times and see how much it stinks, they'll change it back, and by then I'll be too old to enter."

Mark sighed. What was the point? Mark didn't want to listen, and what did *Mark* care if Mark won or lost the contest? In fact, he hoped Mark *did* lose. He needed to realize that he was not automatically the best at everything, that no one thought he was but him. He put his math book in his backpack and stood up.

"Where are you going?" Mark asked.

Mark crossed his arms. "I'm trying to help you out, but you don't care. You think that no one can teach you anything, but really they can and you just won't let them. You *asked* me for help, Mark. I spent a lot of time this week putting together stuff that would help *you* prepare for *your* tournament. But no matter what I say, you just say you know it or it doesn't matter. So there's no point in me staying." He paused to catch his breath, and in doing so realized what he was saying. His eyes grew wide and his ears grew red. "Sorry," he said.

"No," said Mark. His eyes were wide, too. And his mouth was expanding by the second.

"No?"

"No, don't apologize. That was really good. You just defended yourself! You didn't just stay quiet and dumb—no offense. I mean"—Mark burst into his form of a grin—"you weren't shy!"

"I—I guess I wasn't."

Mark laughed. "No, you weren't! If only you had that much . . . conviction with everyone. That was awesome."

Mark smiled. "It was?"

Mark nodded enthusiastically.

Mark laughed. "Yeah," he said. "I know it was."

"Don't you mean 'thank you'?" Mark asked.

Mark laughed harder. "Thank you," he said, but it sounded more like "Ha-th-ha-hoo!"

"You're welcome," Mark spit out through laughs, making them laugh harder.

When Miss Payley came to check on them, she found one Mark Hopper kneeling on the floor, laughing so hard his face was bright red, and the other Mark Hopper roaring with laughter, his head bent back and his hand banging on a desk. She stood in the doorway and watched for a while, a curious smile playing on her lips. Then she said, "I wish all my students had this much fun finding the volume of spheres."

Both Marks looked up. They looked at each other and calmed down a bit.

"It is fun," one Mark said.

"Yeah," said the other. "Thank you for teaching it to us!"

The first Mark snorted.

"You're welcome," said Miss Payley.

The two boys broke down once again. Miss Payley shook her head and went back to the teachers' lounge.

Chapter 21

Mark's Plan Progresses

Both Marks were so busy that the next few weeks passed quickly. They met every Wednesday right after eighth period in Miss Payley's room to study math and learn the basics of teamwork and speaking up. Mark couldn't believe that week after week, no matter how easy the topic was, Mark still needed help understanding the concepts and doing the homework. And Mark couldn't believe that no matter how much he thought he understood the topic, the other Mark made him understand it better and do the homework quicker. And for the most part, the next few weeks passed without a hitch.

Well, for the most part. The Mark who was too shy to speak to teachers, let alone try to be their best friend, once found a note that said "Kiss-up!" stuck to his locker and a group of kids he didn't know running away and laughing. But he just crumpled up the note and pretended it didn't happen. The Mark whose notebooks were filled with gold stars and the letter *A* was called down to his guidance counselor to talk about his failing grades in English and science. But he just promised the guidance counselor he'd do better and offered to check the other Mark's English and science homework after they had finished the math. Many Ivy Road students didn't even realize that there was more than one Mark Hopper, or that there was one who did not match their idea of what Mark Hopper was like. But for those who did know of them both, it seemed as though each Mark had forgotten that the other was ruining his life.

Mark Hopper spent afternoon after afternoon perfecting his portrait of Grandpa Murray. He studied him every chance he could get. One evening when Mark stared at Grandpa Murray as he read the newspaper on the couch, Grandpa Murray looked up and said, "You keep looking at me, Mark. Did I put my pants on backward again?"

Mark carefully redrew the pencil sketch on a canvas (he started one of them too low on the canvas, not leaving room for the coffee table with Grandpa Murray's newspaper, so he had to start over again). He mixed colors and brought the portrait to life with paint. He couldn't help but drop some hints to Grandpa Murray about how great his birthday present was going to be, and he even risked taking the picture home from school one day to show it to Beth. He slid it under his bed so Grandpa Murray wouldn't see it, and when he took it out, it had so much dust on it that he sneezed for five minutes straight. Even though he was still putting the final touches on it, Mrs. Irwin had already given him an A, and she told him that she would display it at the library. Everything was going according to plan.

Mark Hopper spent day after day forcing himself to say "thank you" and "you're welcome." After a few days, he didn't have to force himself. Then he moved on to "that's a really good idea," and "no problem." As the words became more natural, so did his conversations with other people. He spent afternoon after afternoon perfecting his Mastermind tournament entry. He wrote three drafts of his essay, "An Open Mind Opens Doors for the Future" by Mark Geoffrey Hopper. He practiced answering interview questions in front of the mirror ("Well, I never really thought about what I consider to be the most important skill taught in middle school, but if I had to come up with something off the top of my head . . ."). He took his fifth-grade report card out of its frame on his wall, made a color copy, and had it laminated. He practiced his bassoon solo until he could play it by heart, and then he made Beth be totally silent for ten minutes while he played it into the microphone on their computer to make a CD (no matter how strongly Mark argued, his mother refused to pay to have the solo professionally recorded). When it was all done, Mark sat admiring it on his bed. He knew it was a strong application. Very strong. He could probably win the competition with it. But he would *definitely* win the competition if he had one more thing.

Now was the time to put his plan into action. The timing could not have worked out better. Mark had proudly told him that he was going to be completely done with his portrait the next day. And the Mastermind application was due in one week. But now he wasn't sure if he should go through with it. Mark was being so nice to him. He actually liked having Mark as a friend—he actually hoped, sincerely, that Mark considered him a friend—and he wouldn't want to ruin that by having him find out that Mark had stolen from him. But the painting was just going to sit in the art room until it was brought to the library on December 2, and the Mastermind finals were going to take place on December 1 at a college right next to the public library—how else could that be interpreted except as a sign that Mark should go through with it? If he did it right, Mark would never find out. And what couldn't he do right?

But he also knew how hard Mark had worked on the portrait, and how happy he was with how it came out. He wouldn't like it if someone tried to hand in one of his essays as his own; that would be cheating. But that was why he always took extra precautions against cheating, he rationalized. He blocked his paper with his arm in class, and he wrote his name all over his binders and folders. If Mark *really* cared about his painting, he wouldn't go around advertising the fact that as of tomorrow, it would just be sitting in the art room waiting to be moved over to the library to go on display.

At dinner Sunday night, Mark pushed around the french fries on his plate. Since he had the CD of his bassoon performance, his application was technically complete without the painting—one fry to the right. But if he had the portrait, he'd be sure to win—one fry to the left. Mark Hopper would hate him if he found out—one fry to the right. But Mark didn't have to find out—one fry to the left. Mark *wanted* Mark to win—he said it himself—and he was helping him prepare for the teamwork part—two fries to the left.

Beth took one of Mark's fries from the left.

"Hey!"

"If you're just going to count them, then I am going to eat them."

"Mom!"

Mrs. Hopper pointed her finger. But before she could scold Beth, the phone rang and she got up to answer it.

Beth took another of Mark's fries and held it up to her lips like a smile. "Saved by the phone," she said.

"Oh, hi," Mark's mom said into the phone with a tired and sarcastic tone.

Mark jumped up. "Is it Dad?"

His mother nodded and signaled for Mark to wait. She took the phone and moved into the living room. Mark tried to follow, but she pushed him back into the kitchen.

"Is it Dad on the phone?" Beth asked.

"Yeah!"

"I just lost my appetite." Beth spit the fries that were in her mouth, half chewed, onto her plate. "I don't know why you like talking to him so much."

"He's our dad," Mark said.

"But he left us."

"He'll come back."

"I hope not."

"Don't say that."

Beth rolled her eyes. "Things are so much better without him here."

"Shut up!"

Beth sighed. She reached for Mark's shirt and used it to pull him close to her. "All right," she said. "I'm sorry. I know you miss him." She tried to tousle Mark's hair, but it was gelled so tightly that not a strand moved. Beth laughed and pushed him back away. "But really, Mark, don't you remember what it was like when Dad was here?"

"It was great," Mark said firmly.

Their mother appeared back in the kitchen and offered the phone to Mark. He ran into the living room with it and jumped onto the couch. "Hi, Dad!"

"Hey, Mark. How is everything going?"

"Good, Dad. I'm doing really well in school."

"Good." Mr. Hopper's voice sounded distant, as though he was speaking into the phone but looking another way. Mark thought he heard someone else talking the background. It was probably the television. "How's that little friend of yours? What's her name . . . across the street."

"Jasmina?"

"Jasmina. Are you two still friends?"

"Sure," Mark said quickly. "Dad, I'm applying to the Mastermind tournament. My application is all ready to go."

"All right!" his dad said, his voice sounding closer. "Are you going to win?"

"I think so."

"You *think*? You're a Hopper, and this is the Mastermind tournament. You should *know* so."

"Okay, I *know* so. The application is due next week. And then the finalists go December first."

"And when do they give you the trophy?"

Mark puffed up his chest. "That night. December first."

"December first . . . That's a really nice ceremony they do for those awards. I remember when I won it—all three years—I had to give a speech, and they took lots of pictures, and then there was a reception for everyone."

Mark could see it. He'd hear them announce his name, and he'd walk down the aisle of a large auditorium, receive his trophy, and pose with it for pictures. He'd shake everyone's hand and turn down offers to run various companies, saying school comes first, though maybe he could help them out during summer vacation. The newspapers would contact his dad for an interview—to speak to the man who raised such a son, and who won the tournament himself three years in a row—and then his dad would say how proud he was that Mark was his son. "Dad . . ." Mark took a deep breath. "Do you think you could come to the awards ceremony if I win?" Then he held his breath.

"December first? That'd be fun. Maybe."

Mark jumped up on the couch. "Really!"

"Maybe," his father repeated. "Does your sister want to say hello?"

"She's not home," Mark lied.

"All right," his father said. "Okay, well, I need to go, Mark. Let me talk to your mother once more."

"Okay. December first, Dad. Remember."

"All right. Get your mother."

Mark ran back into the kitchen and scooped up the rest of the fries on his plate. He ate them by the handful. Then he ate what was left on Beth's plate, too. Tomorrow was a big day, and he'd need all the energy he could get.

Chapter 22

Mark's Plan Progresses

Almost as much as he was proud of the portrait itself, Mark was proud of his success in hiding it from Grandpa Murray all weekend while he finished it up. He put a piece of paper on his door that read TOP-SECRET BIRTHDAY OPERATION IN PROGRESS. NO GRANDPAS ALLOWED. He and Beth invented a secret-code knock that she and their mother had to use if they wanted to enter his room. And on Sunday night, when Mark was all done, the three of them admired the portrait while Grandpa Murray stood outside the closed door and tried to guess what they were doing.

"It sounds very quiet!" Grandpa Murray said. "So using my expert skills of deduction, I say that my birthday present is *not* an original play that you have to rehearse."

Mark and Beth and their mom laughed as they looked at the painting.

"Now I hear laughing! Is my present a comedy routine?"

"Go away," Mrs. Hopper said. "You'll know soon enough." She signaled for Mark and Beth to be quiet while they waited to see if they could hear Grandpa Murray moving from the door.

"I hear breathing!" Grandpa Murray said after ten seconds. "I think my birthday present involves breathing."

"Go away, Grandpa!"

"Oh, all right." Grandpa Murray went back to the book he was reading, which he was starting from the beginning for the third time in three weeks, since he kept forgetting that he had started it at all, let alone what happened in it.

"This really is very, very impressive, honey," Mrs. Hopper whispered. She kissed Mark on his freckled forehead.

"Yeah, it came out really, really well," Beth agreed.

Mark couldn't stop smiling or keep his ears from turning red. "Thanks. I'm going to bring it in tomorrow, but it's supposed to rain, so can you drive me to school?" he asked his mom.

"Oh, no, sweetie," she said. "I can't take you tomorrow. I have to go to work early. Grandpa can drive you. But you'll have to disguise the painting."

"Disguise it?" Mark asked with wide eyes. He pictured the portrait with a drawn-on black mustache.

"Cover it up," Beth said. "You could put a pillowcase around it."

"Oh," Mark said. "I could just wrap it in some paper and put it in a box. They have to do that to move it to the library anyway."

"I have the box that my insect study kit came in," Beth offered. "That'd be the perfect size." She went to get it, opening the door a crack first to make sure Grandpa Murray was not going to try to sneak in.

"Bring the phone, too, so we can call Dad!" Mark called after her.

"Great idea," his mother said. "He's going to be so impressed with how this painting came out."

"You know who else you should call?" Beth sang when she returned with the box and the phone. "Lau-rie!"

"Laurie? Who's Laurie?" Mrs. Hopper asked with the same singsong tone.

"I told you," Beth said. "The girl we saw at the supermarket. She's going to invite Mark to her birthday party."

"Oh, that's right," their mother said. "Oh, Mark's turning red."

"I don't even really know her," Mark said quietly. "And besides, she hasn't even invited me yet. I haven't even seen her since! I think she was just being nice."

"*Very* nice," Beth said. She held up her hands. "Okay, okay, I'll stop."

Mark took the phone and dialed his father's phone number. Mr. Hopper picked up halfway through the first ring. "Hi, Dad!"

"Mark! I was *just* going to call you guys. I mean *just* going to call you. I had the phone in my hand and my finger just over the number six."

"Really?"

"Well, actually I wasn't going to call to talk to you. I wanted to speak to a couple of Beth's earthworms. And the new slug. I wanted to welcome Sluggo to the family."

"Sorry, the earthworms are busy . . ." Mark said. He tried to think of a science word. "Photosynthesizing."

Beth slapped her freckled forehead. "Bugs don't engage in photosynthesis!" she said. "That's plants!"

Mark shrugged. "Sorry, Dad. Beth says bugs don't do photosynthesis. Sluggo is cool, though. He has just been hanging out on the wall of the tank since this morning."

Beth grinned. Mrs. Hopper winced. Mr. Hopper said, "Cool."

Mark whispered to his dad all of the details of his painting. "And it's going to be on display in the Greenburgh library starting December second, which is perfect because that's Grandpa's birthday."

"All right. I am marking it down in my calendar right now. December second. Mark's prizewinning portrait on display in Greenburgh."

Mark blushed. "It hasn't won any prizes."

"Not yet. Just you wait."

"But I'm the only sixth grader whose painting will be in the show. The rest are seventh or eighth graders."

"That's my Mark. Well, December second I will be there for the grand opening."

"All right!"

"And I may have some news then . . ."

Mark gasped. "Did you get a job here?" he asked, his eyes becoming as round as the buttons on his shirt. "Are you coming to live here finally?" Beth looked over expectantly.

"I'm not saying anything," said Mr. Hopper. "Except that I *may* have some good news when I see you on December second."

Mark said that he would wait for the news, and he reminded himself not to get his hopes up, but it *had* to be that his dad had found a new job and was finally going to live with them for good, not just on weekends. While Beth, his mom, and Grandpa Murray talked to Mr. Hopper, Mark floated around the house thinking about how wonderful it would be once his dad moved in for good.

While Beth helped Mark wrap and pack the painting, she told Mark not to get his hopes up, but then she excitedly confessed that she, too, thought the news must be of a new job close by. "That's only my hypothesis," Beth said, "but really I think there is enough evidence for it to be a full-out theory!"

Mark clearly labeled the box with his full name and the title of his portrait: *Grandpa.* He completed his homework in record time and watched *Wheel of Fortune* with Grandpa Murray before bed. He fell asleep smiling. In the morning, he whistled on the way to school and grinned as he dropped off the box with the portrait before homeroom.

He was still smiling during lunch when he told Jonathan and Mark Hopper that his painting was finished, boxed up, and in the art room waiting to be transported.

Mark Hopper smiled back.

Chapter 23

Mark Hopper: Master Thief

This was going to be easy.

Every Monday afternoon all of the teachers in the whole school had a half-hour meeting in the cafeteria; Mark knew because Mr. Rocco had once told Mark he couldn't discuss the four points Mark lost on a geography quiz on a Monday afternoon because of the teacher meeting, so Mark had waited outside the cafeteria and then argued his case for his four points while running alongside Mr. Rocco on his way from the meeting to his car. Just to be sure Mrs. Irwin would certainly be at the meeting—timing was crucial—Mark spent an extra five minutes at his locker after eighth period playing a game he'd invented that involved seeing how quickly he could organize the binders by subject, then by teacher's last name, then by teacher's first name, then by importance in life. Then he walked casually down to the art room, being sure to say hello to some people on the way and mention that he was heading home—he was setting up his alibi, just in case. He took a deep breath before walking down the art wing, a corridor on the second floor of the school with large windows overlooking a courtyard that was opened once a year for refreshments after the eighth-grade graduation. The corridor smelled like the art room at Farrow Park Elementary School—a warm combination of crayons, paint, and copper pennies—and Mark worried for a moment that someone might be able to pick up the smell on him and question what he was doing in the art wing. He had better make this quick.

The door to the main art room was open and Mark could see a handful of students inside. Some sat in front of easels or hovered over sketchbooks. A few others stood in a corner by what looked like a supply closet, laughing and chatting as they combed the closet for materials. Luckily, Mark didn't recognize any of them. Even more luckily, they all seemed to be older, so they probably didn't know the other Mark.

Mark took a deep breath and walked into the room as though he walked into it every other day for art class. He looked around the room for the boxed-up painting, making sure to look with distinctly Mark Hopper–round eyes, and he thought he spied it in the back by the window.

"Hi," said a boy with black hair and black plastic-rimmed glasses from behind an easel. "Are you looking for something?"

"I think it's right there," Mark said. "I brought in a painting this morning but I realized I want to take it home and work on it a little more."

The boy shrugged and went back to work.

Mark made his way to the box. His name was written in

blocky letters along the top in permanent marker. He reached for the box without the slightest bit of hesitation. It was in his hands. He started back out the door.

"That's the painting of an old man, right?" one of the other painters asked. She pointed at the box. "I kept seeing it in the back of the room. It's *so* good. I love the composition, with the newspaper on the lap, and the door frame to the bedroom in the background."

Mark nodded. "Thank you," he said, just the way Mark would. "I'm glad you like it." He continued toward the door.

"So you're . . ." She squinted at the box. "Mark Hopper, then?"

Mark straightened up and smiled. "Yes," he said truthfully.

"Nice meeting you," the girl said. "Really, really good work on your portrait."

Mark thanked her again and carried the box out of the room. No one else spoke to him. He took the box downstairs, outside, and all the way to the post office. Once there, he opened his backpack and took out the envelope with the other components of his Mastermind application and taped it to the front of the box. He waited in line and mailed the whole package, no questions asked.

Mark Discovers
the Truth

The note was wedged between the slits of Mark's locker door. It had been a week since Mark mailed his Mastermind application, portrait and all, and so far no one had said anything about it to him. But this note got his hands shaking. This was it. He was caught. He envisioned opening the letter to find a message made of letters cut out of magazines and signed with blood: "I saw you take the painting." He imagined having to meet someone under the bleachers after dark with a suitcase full of completed homeworks for the rest of the year in order to keep his secret a secret.

Mark glanced around before taking the note into his hands. His name was printed on the front in round, girlie letters, and it was underlined twice in purple pen. Did blackmailers use purple pen and draw curlicues in their *p*s? Maybe this was just an ordinary note. Back in elementary school he was used to finding notes on top of his books, having been slipped inside his desk surreptitiously. In fifth grade, when he had a desk with a top that opened up, he'd occasionally found a note Scotch-taped to the inside of the top. Once he opened the lid of the desk and a whole scroll unraveled, revealing the word *loser* in multicolored letters. Most of the other notes Mark got had similar messages. Only once had he gotten one that wasn't mean, and that time it was a chain letter that the rest of the class had been talking about for weeks—he was the very last name from his class on the letter—and the girl who'd put it in his desk made it clear to him that she either had to give it to him or risk having bad luck until she got married. "And if I have bad luck until then, I probably won't be lucky enough to get married, so I'll always have bad luck," she explained to Mark. She'd thought about her options thoroughly.

Mark had found a few mean notes in his locker (and once taped to his butt) at the very beginning of the year. But since he'd started being nice and spending time with the other Mark, there had been hardly any. As relieved as he was that the note was probably not an anonymous threat related to his Master- mind crime, he felt his stomach sink at the prospect of getting a mean note. He thought he had come so far. He ripped it open, figuring he might as well read it and get it over with. As though he were the other Mark, his eyes grew wide as balloons when he saw what was inside. A birthday party invitation. To a birth- day party. For someone named Laurie Campbell. The invitation was printed from a computer and was cluttered with graphics of cakes and streamers and candles in a conga line. But there was a handwritten note at the bottom:

Dear Mark,
I know we don't really know each other, but I hope you'll come!

                                                    From, Laurie

Mark had to restrain himself from jumping up and down in the hallway. He *knew* all of his work was paying off. Now that his Mastermind application was in, he had time for friends and birthday parties. Laurie's party would be the perfect start. Everyone would see him there and decide to invite him to theirs. He wondered how many people were going. He hoped Frank Stucco or Pete Dale would walk by right now. Then he would casually ask them if they were going to Laurie Campbell's birthday party. If they said they were, he could just say, "Oh yeah, me too. See you there." And if they said no, then he could say, "Oh, no? Well, I guess I won't see you there!" But it was comments like that that caused him to find rude notes in his locker. It was comments like "good job" and "do you need help?" that got him birthday-party invites—well, just one so far. But he was making progress! He didn't want—what was her name?—Laurie . . . to take back the invitation. He would have to be a perfect gentleman about it. And if he did see Frank or Pete there, they would see him hanging out with everybody, and they'd be jealous of the way Laurie would like his present best. He could picture the scene now . . . except for the minor detail of not knowing what Laurie looked like. And if he didn't see Frank or Pete, then he could say to them the next day in school that it was too bad they weren't there because it was so much fun!

Mark practically glided home, he was so excited. The party

wasn't for almost two weeks, but he wished it was for that night. When he got home, he called his mom at work.

"Is everything okay? Is Beth there with you?" she asked. He hadn't called her at work since the first week of school when she had insisted he call to say he had made it home safely, and Mark had complained that that was baby stuff.

"Yes," Mark said. "I just wanted to make sure you don't have to work on November seventeenth. It's a Saturday."

"I never work on Saturdays."

"Okay," Mark said. "I was just checking."

"Okay," Mrs. Hopper said. "See you later, Mark." She hung up.

Mark hung up the phone angrily. Why couldn't his mother just ask what was on November 17? He could have just found out that he was going to receive the Nobel Peace Prize that day, for all she knew. Or he could have just scheduled an appointment to have his left kidney operated on that day. Or he could have been invited to a birthday party for someone other than a cousin or Jasmina for the first time since he was seven years old, which was just as big of a deal.

Mark picked up the invitation and knocked on Beth's door. "What?" she shouted.

"Can I open the door?" Mark asked.

"Who is it?"

"Oh, come on."

"I don't recognize your voice. I'm not going to invite a stranger into my room! I'm not stupid. I could get murdered!"

"Yeah, because a murderer would knock, moron. And you're pretty stupid if you don't recognize your brother's voice."

The door flew open. "Oh, you're my brother? Why didn't

you just say so?" Beth gave him the signature Hopper smile and popped her gum.

Mark wanted to give her his I-don't-bother-with-idiots look, but it would have involved looking away from the invitation, which he was pretending to read. "Do you know where Orchard Lane is?"

Beth shook her head. "Look it up," she said, before shutting the door.

Mark huffed. "Well, I was just wondering because I was invited to a birthday party at someone's house on Orchard Lane!" he shouted through the door.

Mark waited a whole minute, but Beth didn't respond. His family was good for nothing. He walked over to Jasmina's house and knocked on the door. He saw the ruffle of curtains as someone checked to see who was there before Jasmina herself opened the door. "What's up?" she said.

"Oh, nothing," said Mark casually. "I was just wondering if you know Laurie Campbell."

Jasmina raised her eyebrows. "Why? Do you have a crush on her, too?"

"What? No. Who has a crush on her?"

"Oh, just about everyone." She rolled her eyes and fiddled with one of her braids.

Mark had been invited to the birthday party of someone everyone had a crush on! He felt his heart start beating faster, and worried that Jasmina would be able to somehow see it through his shirt, he crossed his arms. "But you know her?" he asked.

"Yeah. This tall. Long blond hair. Her locker is just around the corner from ours. Kylie has just about every class with her, so we talk sometimes. Why?"

Mark shrugged. "She invited me to her birthday party."

Jasmina hid her surprise, but not so well that Mark didn't notice it. "Cool," she said.

Mark couldn't help but grin. "I know!"

Mark's grin was contagious. "Yeah, not bad," Jasmina said. She patted him on the back. "I told you being nice would pay off." Mark shrugged and stood there grinning, and Jasmina laughed. "Very cool," she said again. "I was invited, too, actually. I wasn't sure if I was going to go, but I'll go if you go."

Mark pretended to consider it for a moment. "Well, all right," he said. "I *guess* I'll go."

After a few seconds, both he and Jasmina burst out laughing.

With having to wait to hear from the Mastermind committee and having to wait to go to the birthday party, the next two weeks passed more slowly than ever. Mark and his mother went shopping for some new dress pants and a nice tie that he could wear if he was a Mastermind finalist. His mother also suggested that they buy a nice sweater for him to wear to the party. He usually just put on whatever she bought him, but this time he went to the store with her and carefully considered each of the sweaters his mother held up, even though they all looked and felt pretty much the same to him. His mom picked out a pair of earrings to give Laurie as a present, and she asked Mark if Laurie would want something else. Mark had no idea—he still wasn't completely sure of which girl with long blond hair was Laurie Campbell, though he'd been trying to figure it out since he got the invitation—but after much thought he decided that he should also get her a copy of his favorite book, *Einstein: A Biography,* in hardcover. He wrapped it himself using the Sunday color comics as wrapping paper—he had seen someone do that in a movie once and thought it was a neat touch.

He wanted to bring up the birthday party every time he talked to anyone, but he decided to keep it a secret. Maybe it was a very exclusive party, and Laurie would get angry if she found out that he was blabbing it all around. He wanted to ask the other Mark about it, but he decided not to unless he brought it up first, just in case he wasn't invited. And when the other Mark didn't bring it up at all, Mark began to wonder if he was invited, too, but was trying not to mention it in case *he* wasn't invited. He thought of one day back in fourth grade when some girls asked Jasmina to join a club they'd formed called the Kewl Girls, and Jasmina made Mark promise not to tell Kylie, who wasn't a member. The Kewl Girls ended up fighting with one another and disbanding into six individual clubs just hours after Jasmina joined, but for the first time Mark understood why Jasmina had wanted to make sure Kylie didn't find out. He realized that if the other Mark *was* invited to Laurie's party and wasn't telling him, he would be happy.

The day of the party finally arrived. Mark woke up early and chatted with his mom excitedly at breakfast. He had so much time that instead of a shower he took a long bath, which had the added benefit of annoying Beth by keeping her locked out of the bathroom for longer. After his bath, he cleaned his ears and brushed his teeth. He put his new gel in his freshly cut hair and made sure each strand was perfect. He wanted to try shaving— he had done it once with his dad with a bladeless shaver—but he didn't have a razor or any shaving cream, and he couldn't feel even a single dot of stubble on his face anyway. He put on his nice dress pants and tucked in his shirt, then put on the new sweater. Looking in the mirror, he knew he looked sharp. Jasmina arrived at one-thirty and she and Mark piled into Mrs. Hopper's car to drive over to Orchard Lane. Jasmina and Mrs. Hopper chatted throughout the five-minute ride, but Mark was too busy trying not to show just how nervous and excited he was to say anything.

Mark and Jasmina jumped out at the Campbells' house, which was marked with balloons wrapped around the mailbox. They walked slowly up to the door, waiting for Mrs. Hopper to pull away before ringing the bell. A girl with long blond hair pulled into a ponytail with a ribbon around it opened the door. Mark had seen her in school. She must have been Laurie Campbell.

"Jasmina! Hi!" Laurie said. "I'm so glad you came."

"Happy birthday, Laurie!" Jasmina said. She gave her a hug.

Laurie hugged back and then glanced at Mark. "What are you doing here?" she asked.

Mark froze. Was that a joke? He chuckled nervously in case it was. "I'm here for your party," he said. He held out his two gifts. "Happy birthday, Laurie!"

Laurie crossed her arms. "Um, thanks. But this party is invite only."

"I—I was invited."

Laurie snorted. "I think I know who I invited to my own party."

Jasmina took Mark's arm and started to step into the house. "You invited him, Laurie," she said. "And I told you we were going to come together."

"You said you were coming with Mark Hopper," Laurie said.

"I am Mark Hopper, stupid," Mark said. He directed it at Laurie, but he didn't know who was stupider, Laurie or himself.

A few other kids had gathered around the door to see what was going on. One of them, a girl Mark recognized from his computer class, giggled and said, "You invited *him*?"

Laurie spun around and assured her friend that she hadn't. "No, I invited Mark Hopper," she explained. She spun back around and looked Mark square in the eye. "Not you."

The crowd inside began to buzz with recognition of what had happened. Some others came to see what all of the excitement was about. Pete Dale stood on a stair to tower over the crowd. When he saw Mark he said loudly enough for anyone who had yet to figure it out, "Laurie invited the wrong Mark Hopper!"

"And he thought the invitation was actually for him?" one girl whispered to another.

"I don't know why," the other whispered back. "Clearly he hasn't been to many birthday parties. Look at his sweater. And at his present."

"Yeah, what is he giving her—a newspaper?"

Mark just stood there, staring at the situation. He hoped that Laurie's wooden porch might actually be quicksand, and that it'd slowly engulf him and close up once he had sunk.

Laurie's parents made their way through the crowd to the door. "What's the problem, honey?" Mrs. Campbell asked.

"I didn't invite him," Laurie said. She waved her hand as though she could shoo Mark away the way she would a mosquito.

"There was a misunderstanding," Jasmina said. She was still holding Mark's arm tightly.

"Well, that's okay," Mrs. Campbell said. She smiled broadly at Mark. "The more the merrier. We've got enough pizza and cake."

"But, Mom," Laurie whined through clenched teeth. "I don't want him here. You don't understand."

"Laurie," warned Mr. Campbell.

Mark had had enough. He pulled his arm back from Jasmina and thrust the presents into Laurie's hands. "Here," he said. He whirled around and stomped off the porch and down the driveway. He could hear some laughter and shushing and a whine of "But it's my birthday." Jasmina ran after him and called his name, but Mark didn't stop. Once he turned the corner, his pace slowed into a lame walk. Jasmina caught up with him a block later holding his presents, but she was kind enough not to say anything. The two walked slowly and silently back to their street, not stopping or speeding up when it started to drizzle.

When they reached their block, Jasmina tried to give Mark a hug, but he pulled away and walked into his house.

"Is that you, Mark?" his mother called from the kitchen.

Beth looked up from her magazine. "What are you doing home already?" she asked as Mark climbed the stairs silently. "Did you realize no one would want you at their birthday party after all?"

Mark whirled around and stared at his sister. He wanted to spit out a poisonous remark, but he couldn't muster it. He turned back around and continued silently to his room, where he collapsed onto his bed facedown and cried quietly into his pillow.

Later that afternoon, after Mark heard his mother talking to someone on the phone—probably Jasmina—Mrs. Hopper knocked gently on the door. Mark didn't respond, but she entered anyway, and she sat at the edge of the bed and rubbed

Mark's back. She didn't say anything, but she slid an envelope onto Mark's nightstand. He opened it after she left.

Dear Mark Geoffrey Hopper,

Congratulations! Due to the quality of your application, the Mastermind Committee is pleased to inform you that you have been selected as a Mastermind finalist. We received a record number of applications this year, and we selected only twelve finalists. You should be extremely proud of yourself.

All of the finalists are invited to complete the remaining part of the competition, a personal interview and a teamwork exercise, on Saturday, December 1, which this year will be hosted by Marius College in Greenburgh. Details are enclosed. We look forward to seeing you in December. Congratulations once more, and good luck in the final round of the competition!

I should just stick with what I'm good at, Mark thought. I should just focus on winning the Mastermind competition. I'm good at getting A's and writing essays and playing the bassoon. Clearly I am, because I am a finalist.

The thought cheered him up, but only slightly, because clearly he was not good at being a person other people like being around. No matter how many "how was your weekend"s and "thanks for your help"s he said, no matter how genuine his smile, no matter how many impolite remarks he stopped himself from saying, he was still the Mark Geoffrey Hopper who reminded the teacher to give the quiz she seemed to have forgotten about, not the Mark Geoffrey Hopper who got invited to birthday parties on purpose. No one liked him. And there was no way he could win the teamwork component if no one liked him.

If I have to do the teamwork part, Mark thought, I am not going to win. The truth weighed heavily on his body, and he sank deeper into his bed. *I'm not going to win.*

From the crack of the door his mother had left open, Mark could see the empty glass shelf where his father's trophies used to be. Not even his own dad liked him enough to stick around. And he was going to fail in the only way he knew to bring him back. He whispered it out loud, his hushed voice sad but certain. "No one likes me, and I'm not going to win."

For the second time that day, Mark cried.

Chapter **25**

Mark Discovers
the Truth

Mark had never seen Mark so glum. When he said hello to him in homeroom, Mark let out a pitiful little huff. And when Miss Frances said, "Welcome to the start of a glorious new week!" like she did every Monday, Mark grunted feebly.

"Gesundheit!" chirped Miss Frances.

"Is everything okay?" Mark whispered.

Mark didn't turn around. "Yeah, fine," he muttered.

Mark ripped off a piece of notebook paper. "Are you sure?" he wrote on it. He folded it up into a rectangle and tapped Mark on the shoulder with it. Mark didn't turn around. Mark tapped again, a little harder. Mark shrugged his hand off. So Mark turned around to Jasmina, his eyes wide with concern, and whispered, "Do you know what's up with Mark?"

Jasmina turned her lips down and nodded. But before she

could say anything, Mark turned around from in front of Mark and gave her a please-don't-say-anything look. If it had been a say-something-and-regret-it-the-rest-of-your-life look, neither Jasmina nor Mark would have been so worried. "I'll tell you later," Jasmina mouthed.

But Mark didn't have to wait until much later.

"Hey, Hopper!" shouted Pete Dale in the hallway after homeroom.

Mark turned around, but he saw Pete was calling after the other Mark.

"I'm having a party on Friday," Pete shouted, "and I just want to make it clear that you are *not* invited!"

Mark turned around and yelled, "You couldn't give me a million dollars to go to a party of yours, buttface!"

"But Laurie Campbell had to give you a million dollars to go away!" Pete called after him. The crowd around Pete snickered, and everyone in the hall turned to look after Mark as he pushed his way toward social studies.

"Shut up, Pete," said Jasmina. Her expression was one of pity, not for Mark but for Pete.

"Oh, look," said Pete. "Jasmina is standing up for that loser."

"Just shut up," Jasmina said. She spun around and rolled her eyes at Mark before walking confidently into the girls' bathroom.

"Be careful, Horace!" Frank Stucco yelled after Jasmina. "Mark Hopper might think he's invited and follow you in there!"

Pete and the others roared. "Hey, Hopper," Pete said, signaling toward the Mark who was watching the scene from the side. "*You* probably *are* invited into the girls' bathroom!"

"Yeah," said Frank. "You'd better hurry up in there before the other Mark goes in instead."

Mark stared at the floor and gritted his teeth. He wasn't exactly sure of what was going on, but clearly Mark had done something that made everyone but Jasmina make fun of him. That meant just as much trouble for him from the people who thought *he* was the Mark Hopper who was supposed to be pushed into lockers and given wedgies. But he found that he didn't care what Mark had done to further damage their shared reputation; he cared about Mark. Mark took a deep breath and silently commanded himself to stand up for Mark the way Mark was teaching him to. He opened his mouth. He wasn't sure of what was going to come out, but he hoped it would be venomous. "Stop it," he said forcefully.

Pete looked up from the headlock Frank had him in. "What?" he said.

Mark prayed Pete could not somehow see the knot in his stomach or sense the sweat on his hands. "I said stop making fun of Mark."

"Aw," said one of the girls in the group. "He's sticking up for him."

"Aw, how cute," said Frank Stucco. His voice was sticky like pancake syrup.

The bell rang to signal the start of first period. Mr. Portman, a stern-looking biology teacher with a sharp crew cut, stepped into the hallway. "That was the bell," he said. "What is going on here?"

Pete and Frank disappeared down the hall. Mark stared up at Mr. Portman, his pulse still racing from his brief encounter. "What happened?" Mr. Portman asked. From inside his classroom, bodies were stretched out of their desks and craned toward to door. He knew Mark would have told Mr. Portman what was going on. Mr. Portman towered over him. "What's your name?"

"Mark Hopper."

"Okay, Mark Hopper. Get to class, or I'll give you detention. That goes for the rest of you, too," Mr. Portman said. He walked back into his room to get a pack of detention slips.

Mark and the rest of the crowd hurried away.

"That's Mark Hopper?" Mark heard one girl ask another.

"Yeah," said the girl. "He showed up at Laurie Campbell's birthday party in a suit!"

"Even though he wasn't invited?"

"Yeah."

"He found an invitation in a garbage can and thought that meant he could go," a third girl explained. "And he wasn't wearing a suit. It was a tuxedo!"

"Did you hear that?" Mark heard an older boy say to another around the corner. "Some kid named Mark Hopper crashed Laurie Campbell's birthday party, wearing a polka-dotted bow tie—and her dad threw him out with the trash!"

"Oh yeah, I know," the boy said. "But the dad didn't throw him out. They had to call the police."

"Really?"

"Yeah. My mom's friend's son goes to karate with someone whose friend was there."

"Wow."

Though the story became more and more exaggerated as the day wore on (by third period, Mark had reportedly gotten down on one knee and recited a haiku inside Laurie's living room before being dragged away to spend the night at a mental institution), Mark figured he had a good idea of what had happened. So Laurie did invite me to her party after all! he thought during math, absentmindedly doodling a smiling face. But he felt guilty the moment he thought it. How was Mark supposed to know the invitation wasn't meant for him? Why did Laurie have to be so mean? He was sorry he had ever wanted to be invited in the first place. He gave the doodled face V-shaped eyebrows and pointy teeth. He wondered why Mark never mentioned that he had been invited. Had he not wanted to hurt Mark's feelings in case he hadn't been invited, too? Mark stopped drawing and looked over at Mark, who was slumped so far into his seat he might slide under the desk. Even though it didn't look like it right then, Mark really had come a long way.

Before lunch, Mark found a note on his locker. Inside it read, "A NON-invitation just for Mark Hopper. You are NOT invited to Jimmy's Burger Shack after school today. OR TOMORROW!! So DON'T come!!!" A few girls who were chatting nearby shushed one another when Mark opened it, then ran away giggling and crashing into one another once he looked up.

Mark crossed his arms. When you mess with Mark Geoffrey Hopper, he thought, you mess with Mark Geoffrey Hopper.

Chapter 26

Mark's Proposal

Mark, Jasmina, and Jonathan walked around the whole perimeter of the library before they finally found Mark at a desk by a rack of paperback books. Mark tapped him on the shoulder. "My sister has a lot of slimy, crawly things."

Mark looked up from the social-studies questions he was working on. He had chosen to spend lunchtime in the library doing homework to avoid having to talk to people. "What are you doing here?" he asked, secretly glad Mark was there.

"He came to tell you that his sister has a lot of bugs," said Jasmina from behind him. Mark turned and saw her and Jonathan.

"I know it's weird," Mark explained. "But she really likes bugs."

"And we were thinking we should put some in Pete's locker!" Jonathan said.

Mark raised his right eyebrow. He had gotten many people in trouble over the years, but never himself. But this might not be a bad time to start. "Maybe Frank's locker, too," he said.

"Oh, definitely," Mark agreed. He and the others sat down. "And Laurie Campbell's, obviously."

Mark looked away quickly, but not quickly enough that Mark didn't see him blush. Mark ripped a piece of paper out of Mark's binder and drew a quick picture of a group of snails. "I say snails for Frank," he said. He wrote Frank's name next to the snails. "Since Frank's kind of round and slow."

Mark couldn't help but let out a laugh. A librarian looked over at them with a finger to her lips.

"And how about spiders for Pete?" Jasmina whispered. "No, knowing him he probably likes spiders."

"We could do ants, though!" Mark said. "I think Beth was planning on letting one of her ant farms loose next weekend anyway. We can let them loose in Pete's locker!"

Mark looked at the earnest expressions on his friends' faces. He imagined the look on Pete's face when he opened his locker and found it teeming with little black ants. They could spill some soda on his binders first so that the ants congregated, and then every time Pete turned a page during the day, he'd find more ants. "What about Laurie?" Mark asked.

"Mosquitoes!" Jonathan cooed.

"Good one," said Mark, his eyes as round as the mosquito bites he had gotten all over his legs when he and Sammy had gone camping with their dads. "Then she won't be able to forget about it for a long time . . . at least until the bites stop itching."

Mark thought about the time a few summers ago when his family went hiking and he pointed out a clump of poison ivy to Beth. She accused him of lying and rolled in the ivy to prove it . . . and her whole body looked lobsterlike within the hour. He pictured Laurie red with bites everywhere from her ears to her ankles, including out-of-the-way places like behind her knees and beneath her toes. He pictured her with too many itches for her pink polished nails to scratch.

Mark tapped Mark on the shoulder with his pencil and pointed to a sketch he was drawing. The cartoonish figure looked *just* like Laurie Campbell running from a swarm of angry mosquitoes.

"I'm a finalist in the Mastermind tournament," Mark said quietly.

"Hey! Congratulations!" Mark said cheerily. "That's so cool."

"Mark!" said Jasmina. "That's awesome." She patted him on the back.

"I don't know what that is," Jonathan said. "But it sounds really important, so good job."

"Thanks," Mark whispered. He thought about the painting and a bowling-ball-size lump formed in the pit of his stomach. He didn't like stealing from Mark when he did it, but now he felt absolutely miserable about it, since Mark was here, cheering him up and offering his sister's insects for revenge. What made it even worse was the fact that it was all for nothing, since he had no chance of winning the teamwork part.

"Okay," said Jasmina. "I need to go eat. Come down to the cafeteria, Mark. I'll buy you a chocolate milk to celebrate."

"Yeah, let's go to lunch," said Jonathan.

Mark shrugged.

Mark was worried. If being a Mastermind finalist didn't make Mark feel better, nothing would, except for maybe winning the whole contest. "We'll meet you there," he said to Jasmina and Jonathan. Once they'd left, he said to Mark, "We'd better get going on practicing the teamwork part. I thought of a lot more games to tell you about, and tricks on what the teachers are looking for when you do them." He raised his eyebrows a few times.

Mark shook his head. "I'm not going."

"What?"

"I'm not going to the finals."

"What do you mean? Why not? You *love* the Mastermind tournament. You've been talking about it forever, and you've been preparing for it for longer than forever."

"Well, it was a waste of time, okay?" Mark snapped. The librarian looked over at them again and shook her head sternly. Mark did not have the energy to return her glare with a sterner one. "I'm not going to win the teamwork part. I know I can't."

"Sure you can," Mark said as convincingly as he could. "I mean, it's probably not your *strongest* part, but that's why I'm helping you."

"I won't, okay? I know I won't. So don't bother telling me I will."

"Okay, well, that doesn't mean that you shouldn't *go* to the final round at all. There's the interview," Mark pointed out. "You'll do really well in that. And then you'll just do the teamwork part, using the tips we've been talking about." Mark only grunted and turned away in response, so Mark continued. "The teamwork stuff really is easy, Mark. There's this one game where everyone gets a picture from a story and you have to put the story in order but you can't show anybody else your picture. I'm really good at that one. It must be easy if *I'm* good at it," he joked.

Mark, who was facing the rack of paperback books, stopped spinning the rack absentmindedly and began thinking about what Mark was saying.

"I'll do whatever I can to help you," Mark continued. "We'll work really hard until the tournament. You worked too hard to drop out now. Someone named Mark Hopper needs to win."

I did work really hard, Mark thought. And someone named Mark Geoffrey Hopper should win. Both of us want Mark Geoffrey Hopper to win. . . . "Well, I guess we can just practice a lot," he said slowly.

"Yeah! All right!"

"But you know I just don't have a chance."

"Well . . ."

"I wish you could just go and do that part for me." Mark laughed.

Mark laughed, too. Then he widened his eyes.

Mark tried not to smile.

"Well," the wide-eyed Mark said. He lowered his voice to an even softer whisper. "I probably *could* go and do it for you. I *am* Mark Geoffrey Hopper."

Mark pretended to find this idea a surprise. "Oh yeah," he said. "They don't know what I'm supposed to look like. They just check your school ID when you get there." He knew that this— if they did it—was *really* cheating. Not that submitting Mark's painting wasn't cheating, but this somehow seemed worse. Sending someone in your place . . . Beth had told him about a guy named Derek Sanford who hired somebody to pretend to be him and take the SATs in his place. But they got caught because the proctor that day happened to be Derek's neighbor, and both Derek and the hired guy got expelled from school, and it went on their permanent records that they were cheaters, and it ruined their lives forever. (Once, when they were on a trip to New York City, Beth pointed to a large, bushy-haired homeless man who was sitting on the side of the street and mumbling to himself and said, "That's Derek Sanford!" Mark thought she was lying— how would she really know?—but he wasn't one hundred percent sure.) But Derek Sanford was stupid to send someone who wasn't also Derek Sanford, and that was why they got caught. If any of the Mastermind judges knew either of the Mark Hoppers, how would they realize that the one there was the wrong Mark Hopper? It was foolproof. And if he won, his dad would come to the awards ceremony, and then Mark could convince him to move back home. Mark took a deep breath. This part was the hardest to say. "If you did go, I bet anything you would win. You've done all this weird teamwork stuff before, and you were good at it. You're nice to everybody . . . even to *me*. And more importantly, everyone likes you," he said. "If someone doesn't, it's only because they think you're me." He sighed.

Mark looked at Mark with his mouth tightened in a combination of pity, nervousness, and excitement. "I don't know about that last part," he said, shrugging one shoulder. "But I *have* done the teamwork stuff." He shook his head. His going to the tournament pretending to be Mark was a crazy idea. He felt guilty just thinking about it, even if he was good at teamwork games. "It's cheating, though!" he hissed, sneaking a quick glance at the librarian.

"But how would they ever know?" Mark pointed out. "You said someone named Mark Hopper deserves to win. And it won't be me if you don't help."

"But then I'd have to do the interview, too . . ." Mark said. "And I wouldn't be any good at that." That was true, and he figured it was a good enough reason to dismiss the whole idea before he might start considering it seriously.

Mark's leg began to shake. Mark was considering it! "Oh, that's no problem," he said. "You've gotten so much better. You're almost not shy at all. I'll help you prepare some more. And adults like you, so you'll be fine."

Mark sighed. He knew how much winning the tournament meant to Mark. And even more than that, he knew how much having a real friend—one who would do anything to help him— meant to Mark. Jasmina couldn't go to the tournament in his place, so she didn't count. Mark had really helped him raise his math grades. And he did like playing teamwork games; he was great at them. The interview would be tough, but it was a good challenge for him to work toward. He glanced around the library furtively. Then he grabbed a paperback and opened it. He whispered to Mark from behind the book, "When is the tournament?"

"December first," Mark whispered back.

"You're sure it's not the second? That's the day my painting is going up in the library, and I'm taking Grandpa Murray to go see it. And my dad will be in town, too."

"My dad said he'd come to the awards ceremony!" Mark said excitedly. He didn't say anything about the painting. "Of course"—he shrugged—"that's only if I win."

"What time? My dad is getting in that afternoon."

"It starts at eleven," Mark said. "And only goes for about two hours."

Mark did some calculations, which Mark thought took him far too long, but he kept quiet about it. Finally, Mark spoke, and his eyes widened with surprise at his own words: "Okay, I'll do it."

Mark grinned. "Thank you," he said sincerely. He thought about the painting and wondered if he deserved such a good friend. Mark was willing to cheat to help him, and Mark was now cheating twice to help himself. "You know," he said, "you're the best friend I ever had. Probably a better friend than I deserve."

Mark shrugged and took a deep breath. "Now what about those bugs?" he said.

Chapter 27

Team Hopper Prepares

The rain was coming down by the bucketful the afternoon of November 21. Mark and Mark stood in the lobby of Ivy Road Middle School, staring out the window at the downpour and waiting for Grandpa Murray to come pick them up. It was time to plan Operation: Mastermind.

Mark didn't know what to expect from Mark's grandpa, even though he had seen the drawing of him. He wondered if Grandpa Murray would be like a television grandfather, one who took Mark fishing and taught him to play chess. Or maybe he'd be one of those movie grandfathers who spoke grandly and said wise things. Mark had two grandfathers, but neither of them ever took him fishing or spoke grandly. He had never even met Grandpa Charlie; he used to imagine what he might be like from his handwriting on Christmas and birthday cards, but those stopped coming even before Mark's dad left. The other, Grandpa John, was very old and smelly, and whenever the Hoppers visited, he didn't even get up from his old and smelly armchair in his older and smellier apartment. Grandpa John had a full-time nurse who tried to be funny by asking Mark how old he was and saying, "But you're sure you're not thirty-five?" when he answered her. Once, Mark asked the nurse how old *she* was, and his mother yelled at him so loudly that the people in the apartment downstairs started banging on the ceiling with a broomstick.

Grandpa Murray's enormous, boxy car looked more like a boat than a car driving up to the school. And he did drive up to the school: over the curb, onto the pavement, and right up to the string of doors. "Oh, geez." Mark laughed. "I told you he was crazy. Come on."

The other Mark muttered, "Does he know how to drive?" He debated walking in the storm, but Mark had already hopped into the boat of a car and was waving through the open door for him to jump in, too.

"How'd you like that door-to-door service?" Grandpa Murray asked as he reversed down the curb and back onto the street.

"First-class," said Mark.

Mark didn't say anything.

"Where to, men?"

"Home please, driver," said Mark.

"Are you sure you don't want to make any pit stops?" Grandpa Murray asked. "For an ice cream cone maybe? Or a movie? It's a good day for a movie."

"But it's a school night," Mark said incredulously.

"Ah, I forgot," Grandpa Murray said with a wink.

"It's Wednesday," Mark said.

"You're right. Express service to the Hopper residence, then."

"Thanks for picking us up, Grandpa."

"Of course. But I really only did it to try to get some information out of this young man about my top-secret birthday present."

"Then you wasted your time," Mark said. He motioned for Mark to keep quiet. "Mark has been briefed, and if he lets even one detail leak, he will suffer grave consequences."

"Okay, okay," Grandpa Murray said. "So, um, Mark. Will I like all of the songs on the CD Mark made me for my birthday?"

Mark started to say "What CD?" but caught himself. "Good try," he said to Grandpa Murray.

"You kids are no fun. I have no choice but to be no fun in return." He refused to talk the rest of the short drive home, even when Mark prodded him by asking questions about Murray's favorite TV game shows and saying things like "Grandpa, tell Mark about the time you won the turkey-eating contest."

Once they reached Mark's house, Mark took Mark to his room and closed the door. "Thanks for keeping quiet about the painting," he said. "It's a surprise because his birthday is on December second, which is when the painting will be in the library."

"So you're going to take him to see it?"

"Yeah, I just have to figure out a way to get him to the library. It will look kind of suspicious if I just want to go, but if my sister's in on it, it'll be really easy. She goes to the library all the time. It's like she lives there." Mark looked around. "But speaking of figuring things out . . ."

Mark nodded. He took out a piece of paper and a pen. The other Mark closed his door gently but firmly. They both dropped their voices. "Operation: Mastermind," Mark whispered.

"Okay," Mark said. "I double-checked all of this information. The competition starts at eleven o'clock on Saturday, the first. But registration is from ten-thirty till eleven. That's going to be the toughest part. Once you're through registration, you'll be in the clear."

"Oh yeah," Mark whispered back, unconvinced. "Sure." In the clear except for the whole competition, he thought.

"So when you sign in, they'll probably check two things: my—well, your finalist letter, which I brought for you, and your school ID."

"Should we switch school IDs?" Mark asked. He took out his ID from his backpack and looked at his freckled face and toothy smile.

"No, why would we switch?" Mark said more sharply than he intended.

"Because I'm supposed to be you."

"But the whole point is you *are* me. Your ID has my name on it and your picture, right?"

Mark checked just to make sure. It said *Hopper, Mark Geoffrey.* "Yes . . . well, *our* name," he said slowly.

"Right, sorry. Our name. So that's perfect. Think about it."

Mark thought. "All right," he whispered finally.

"Okay, so you check in and get your name tag. Then you'll go into a room with all of the other finalists—there are twelve total—and wait there for a little. They'll give you candy and stuff."

"Candy! Are you sure you don't want to go?"

Mark rolled his eyes. "You can eat my share of the candy."

"Okay."

"Okay, so then at eleven you'll start to do the teamwork stuff while the judges look on."

"How do you know the whole schedule?" Mark asked.

Mark shrugged. "I called and asked them for it."

Mark nodded like he himself had just called a store to speak to the manager that morning, when really he was amazed that Mark had had the guts to call and ask all of these questions all by himself.

"So anyway, after the teamwork part, you go one by one to do interviews."

"How long does the interview last?"

"Only about fifteen minutes."

"Only?" Mark said, his eyes as round as capital Os. Fifteen minutes of just him talking to a whole group of adults without Beth or his mom or an excuse to go into the other room was like a whole lifetime. Maybe if he talked really quickly, it would be over in ten.

"Well, it used to be longer," Mark said. "Like twenty-five or a half hour. But now that they're doing that stupid—that teamwork thing, they are spending less time on interviews."

I guess I lucked out then, Mark thought. But then he realized that if there was no teamwork part, he wouldn't be doing this anyway. "What do I do while I wait to be interviewed?"

"Just wait," Mark said. "I think they have all of the artistic stuff on display in another room—" He stopped himself. Mark couldn't go look at the artistic entries or else he'd see his own painting. "But you should just stay put and focus on preparing for the interview," he added quickly. "If they call you and you're not there because you're in another room, then you lose your chance to interview, and then we'll lose," Mark lied. He hoped he sounded convincing. "Plus, they give you lunch in there. And you should be toward the beginning because they go alphabetically."

"Hmm, okay. What was your artistic talent?"

"Bassoon," Mark said.

"Is that like a tuba?"

Mark stopped himself from telling Mark to look it up. "No, it requires far more skill. I'll show it to you one day this week."

"They won't ask me to play anything on it, will they?" Mark asked, scared.

"They can't if you don't have one with you. Which you won't, because it takes years to learn to play the bassoon, and I'm really advanced at it for my age."

Even though Mark figured Mark was just being himself and probably wasn't as good at the bassoon as he purported to be, he still prayed a member of the committee wouldn't reach below his chair, come up with a large instrument, and say, "Oh, what do you know. I just happen to have a bassoon here, so why don't you play a piece or two for us? You can warm up with some scales if you'd like. How about F major?"

"Also," Mark said to cover his tracks, "I put on my application that I like to draw and paint, so if they ask you about that, you can talk about it."

Mark looked at him in surprise. "You like to draw and paint?" he asked. "But you're not in art, are you?"

"No, band."

"You should join art club!" Mark said excitedly. "It's so much fun. I can't believe I never knew you liked to draw. What do you like to draw?"

"Oh, you know. Regular things," Mark said quickly. "Anyway, after the interview you can leave, and the awards ceremony is at night, so I'll go to that and let you know if we win."

"What if," Mark said slowly, thinking his latest fear through, "what if the people at the awards ceremony are the judges? And we win. And you go up to get the award and they say you're not Mark Hopper?"

"Hmm. That's actually a good question," Mark said, impressed. "Well, I am pretty sure that Judy Shane presents the award, and she is obviously too busy to be a judge." Mark could tell that Mark had no idea who Judy Shane was. "Judy Shane is a congresswoman."

"Oh, right," Mark said as earnestly as he could. "*That* Judy Shane."

Mark shrugged. "Well, if it's Judy Shane, we won't have a problem. But if some of the judges are there, too, I think I will just wear really nice clothes and gel my hair like I usually do and everything, and then they will just think, 'Wow, Mark Hopper really looks a lot more handsome when he is all cleaned up.' That should work."

Mark wasn't convinced.

"And if they say I'm not Mark Hopper, I'll just pull out *my* school ID and prove that I am."

Mark could just see Mark getting worked up and yelling at the judges that *of course* he was Mark Hopper, any idiot would be able to see that from his ID. Unless he, too, threw a fit during the final round, then they'd probably be onto them.

"Well, that's not your problem anyway," Mark said, "because you won't be there. I'll figure it out. You just make sure I win. Oh, I almost forgot!" He slapped his forehead. "Getting there. How are you going to get to Marius College? We're so lucky it's right in Greenburgh this year. Last year it was all the way on the Eastern Shore."

Mark had thought about that. "I think I'll have Grandpa Murray give me a ride. I'll tell him it's part of his top-secret present, so I can't tell him why, just that I need to get there."

"We've got this. We are Mark Geoffrey Hopper, Masterminds. Perfect."

Yeah, Mark thought. Perfect, but not easy, or honest, or right. But it was too late to back out now. He might as well turn his attention to something else that wasn't honest but was a lot more fun. "Let's go see if Beth is home yet. We need to talk about bugs."

Operation: Bug Dump

Though Mark and Mark usually dressed similarly, they dressed extra similarly the day before Thanksgiving. They wore khaki pants and tucked-in, blue, collared shirts to match their eyes. Mark still gelled his hair, and Mark still didn't, but they both parted their hair, as usual, on the side, and had, as usual, freckles splattered across their faces. They still didn't really look alike side by side, but with their matching outfits and features, there was pretty much no way to describe Mark to someone else without also describing the other Mark, and vice versa.

Unlike Operation: Mastermind, which needed to be planned and executed in secrecy by only Mark and Mark, Operation: Bug Dump had a crew of seven. Jasmina and Jonathan were excited to be part of the mission, which was deemed a good plan for revenge even by Jasmina, who preferred to settle things with words rather than with tricks. Mark and Mark also requested help from Beth and Beth; Beth for the bug part—she donated an old ant farm and various insects for the cause—and Beth for the dump part—she was a self-proclaimed master at pulling pranks at Ivy Road Middle School. Finally, they brought Grandpa Murray on board, for they and the bugs needed a ride to school from someone who wouldn't ask any questions. Grandpa Murray asked only one question: "If I promise to immediately forget the answer, can you tell me why you are bringing an ant farm, a jar of mosquitoes, and two containers of fruit flies to school?" Mark answered him honestly, and Grandpa Murray patted him on the back proudly before promptly forgetting he had even asked, as promised.

Grandpa Murray drove Mark, Mark, Jasmina, and Jonathan to school at seven-fifteen on Wednesday morning. ("Unless your prank is on the teachers," Beth taught them matter-of-factly, "the best time for pranks at that dumb school is between seven-fifteen and seven twenty-five. Most of the teachers are already there and in their rooms, so you don't have to worry about them catching you. Early-morning detention is already under way, but the students don't really start arriving until seven-thirty.") Even though Beth had drawn out a detailed blueprint of Ivy Road and marked obscure entrances and exits, one of which connected to a secret, underground corridor that was occupied by only janitorial supplies and an extended family of mice, Grandpa Murray dropped them off at the regular front entrance so as not to arouse suspicion. Mark and Mark went to their own lockers, casually, while Jasmina and Jonathan casually scoped out the hallways where Frank's and Laurie's lockers were.

Having taken Mark's painting and never gotten caught, Mark felt like a trained and practiced miscreant. He opened his own locker and placed his backpack on the ground in front of it. He took out a PROPERTY OF MARK GEOFFREY HOPPER. PRIVATE AND NONE OF YOUR BUSINESS folder from the top shelf and placed it in the crook of his left arm, on top of another folder—which was bulky from the ant farm inside. With his right hand, he took his thermos from his backpack. Then he walked over to Pete Dale's locker, which was just a few panels down. Glancing around as though looking for a room that he thought might be in the hallway, Mark made sure no one was coming. He set the two folders down gently and unscrewed the cap of the thermos. It was half full with apple juice. He lifted it to the slits in the locker—the same slits in which the invitation to Laurie's birthday party had been crammed in his locker a few weeks ago—and poured it, just a little bit, into the crack. He heard some of the juice hit the metal bottom of the locker, and a small stream actually started to drip out of the bottom. Mark smiled. He dipped his pinkie finger in the juice and then stuck it into one of the slits and rubbed the juice around the inside, to give the ants a starting place inside the locker rather than out. Satisfied, he took a short swig of the juice, screwed the cap back on, set it down on the ground, and glanced around once more.

Still seeing that the coast was clear, he picked up his folders. Without even opening the bottom one, he opened a corner of the ant farm the way Mark's sister had showed him and started to shake it into the cracks. Some of the sand poured into the locker. "Come on, you stupid little ants," Mark muttered, shaking the farm. "You're free. Free!" As if they could understand, the ants began falling out of the farm along with the sand. "There you go, dummies," Mark whispered. "Follow the apple juice. The sweet, sticky apple juice. Yummy." Some big ones crawled out to follow their friends. A few began crawling on the outside of the locker, and that gave Mark an idea. He knelt down and dumped more of the farm out onto the stream of juice that had dripped through the bottom. The ants scurried around like lunatics, but once they got their bearings they began following the juice trail . . . right through the crack at the bottom and into the locker.

Mark glanced around once more and kept himself from cackling. He quickly closed the farm back up and gathered all of his stuff. He gave Pete's locker his best that's-the-last-time-you'll-mess-with-me look before leaving to walk to the hall with the science labs, where he discreetly dropped the ant farm into the garbage bin that Beth had told him got emptied on Wednesdays and Fridays.

Jasmina was waiting for him there, leaning against a water fountain and trying so hard to look casual she looked asleep. She had worn all black for the occasion, and she'd pulled back her tiny braids into a ponytail so that they wouldn't make noise as she walked. "Oh, hey," she said, feigning surprise at seeing Mark in that hallway. With a large shrug and a big yawn, Jasmina delivered the code they had prepared to signal that the hallway with Laurie's locker was clear: "I just went by Kylie's locker, but she's not here yet." Then she glanced around the empty hall and winked at Mark.

Mark rolled his eyes. If he ever decided to continue his criminal ways, he would not ask Jasmina to join his band of outlaws. "See you in homeroom," he said.

Jasmina looked at him to make sure he understood the code. Mark gave her a yes-I-got-it-five-minutes-ago look. Jasmina watched him make his way briskly toward Laurie's locker before leaving to go to her own.

The hallway was still empty when Mark reached Laurie's locker, but it was 7:24, so he needed to be quick. He removed one arm from his backpack and swung it around on the other shoulder to open it and remove the jar of mosquitoes. This was going to be a little trickier. Once again, he spilled some apple juice inside, and then, to get rid of the last of the juice, he poured some into the locker next to Laurie's, which belonged to a girl whose name he didn't know but whose laugh and whisper he could recognize across the most crowded hallway. He lifted the jar to look inside. A few of the mosquitoes were lying on the bottom, dead, while most of them were lounging around the slice of potato Beth had put in there. One was zooming around frantically, ricocheting off the sides. Mark thought he heard footsteps down the hall. He stuffed the jar into his sleeve and looked back. The boys' bathroom door was swinging closed. Quickly, he removed the jar, unscrewed the lid, and covered the top with his hand. No mosquitoes escaped, not even the wild one, which was now bouncing up and down against his hand. Mark murmured to himself, "One, two, three!" and in one swift motion, removed his hand and pushed the jar up against the locker. He did it a little too forcefully, and the *ding* resounded throughout the hall. (He could imagine Jasmina, around the corner, jumping out of her skin.) A couple mosquitoes flew out and around Mark, though many of them began to buzz around the outside of the locker, trying to find a way in. He pushed a few in, and, presumably having found the apple juice, they didn't come out. Others found their way to the juice on the next locker. This time Mark did let himself laugh.

A toilet flushed, and Mark capped the lid on the jar and dropped it into his backpack. He was about to run away when he heard the bathroom door open, so he began to turn the dial on Laurie's lock instead. A boy came out of the bathroom, whistling. Mark stole glances at him while pretending to look through his backpack. The boy walked to a locker one panel over from where Mark was and began to unlock it. Mark panicked. He couldn't just stand there pretending this was his locker when he didn't know the combination! The boy glanced at him and gave him a head nod, which probably meant he didn't know who he was. Mark spun the lock once more, forcefully, tugged on it as though to make sure it was locked, and walked the other way. Hopefully the boy didn't get a good look at him.

And hopefully he didn't see the mosquitoes circling Mark's head or fingers as he walked away.

Meanwhile, at a corner on the opposite side of the building, Jonathan was standing guard while Mark stood poised in front of Frank Stucco's locker. Frank's locker was easy to spot, for he had engraved FRANK ROCKS in it with the pointy end of a compass. Mark unzipped his backpack and placed it on the floor in front of him. He opened his small carton of orange juice and stuck a bendy straw in it. He took a sip through the straw and placed his finger over the hole. The juice stayed in as he lifted the straw out of the carton and slid the tip of it into the slit in the locker, just above the letter N. He bent the straw so that it was aimed toward the center of the locker. And then, with a glance at Jonathan, who grinned and gave him a thumbs-up, Mark released his finger and jiggled the straw to scatter the juice all over. His eyes were wide, his heart was pounding, and his hands were shaking, which only scattered the juice more. He took the straw out and repeated the process twice more. He was doing it one last time to ensure that Frank's books—or whatever he had in there—were properly juiced, when the straw slipped from his fingers and fell into the locker. "Oh no," Mark said aloud.

"What?" Jonathan whispered from his post at the corner.

"I dropped the straw," Mark said.

"Don't worry about it."

"But it has my fingerprints on it. And my DNA and everything!"

Jonathan shrugged. He gasped. Someone was coming down the hall. "Becky Tummelstein is coming!" he hissed.

Mark froze.

"Quick!" Jonathan said.

"What do I do?" The juice carton was on the floor next to his open backpack, the straw was inside the locker, and a jar of fruit flies was in each of his hands.

"Hey, Jonathan," said Becky. "What are you doing here so early?" She stopped and leaned against the wall by the stairwell. If she took three steps around the corner, she would be able to see Mark, fruit flies and all.

"Oh, hey. What are *you* doing here so early?" Jonathan took a step closer to Becky.

She took a step back. "My sister got early-morning detention, and my mom only wanted to drive here once, so it was either walk here in the freezing cold or come early and just hang out."

"I didn't know you had a sister who goes here."

Becky liked to talk—she frequently got in trouble for it during class—but even so, Mark knew he had no time to waste. He unscrewed the lids on the first jar of flies hastily . . . so hastily that he didn't have a chance to make sure the flies went into the locker. All but a few escaped and flew straight to the light on the ceiling. Whoops, Mark thought. By the time he stopped looking up at the light, all but two fruit flies had escaped into the hallway. He held the jar up to the slits and tapped on the bottom until the last two flew, reluctantly, into the dark locker. He quickly unscrewed the top on the second jar, and this time he held it right up against the locker. Still, about a quarter of the flies managed to squeeze their way out of the sides and into the hallway.

Mark heard Becky talking to Jonathan. "Well, it's seven twenty-five now, so I might as well go to my locker and just go to homeroom."

"What homeroom are you in?" he heard Jonathan ask somewhat desperately.

Mark threw the empty jars into his backpack, grabbed it, and zipped down the hallway. He heard Becky say, "Ew! Flies!" right before he turned the corner.

Up on the third floor, on the opposite side of the building, he met Jonathan, who was flushed.

"You made it?" Jonathan asked quietly.

"Barely," Mark whispered back. He grinned. "Way to hold up Becky!"

Jonathan laughed. "I just kept trying to keep her talking. Usually I can't wait for her to stop talking. It was really backward."

"We're not done yet," Mark said. He held up his backpack.

"Oh yeah," said Jonathan. "I'll do it."

"Nah," Mark said. "I'll do it. I kind of want to see what's in there anyway."

"Let's both do it, then," Jonathan said.

"Okay."

"One," said Jonathan.

"Two," said Mark.

"Three!" they both said. They pushed open the door to the girls' bathroom. It looked disappointingly like the boys' bathroom, except there were more stalls and no urinals.

"I thought there'd be blow-dryers and stuff," said Mark.

"Me too!" Jonathan confessed. "Or at least flowers or something."

In homeroom, Jasmina slipped Mark a note that said, "Code blue?" That was code for, "Did everything go smoothly?" Mark turned around and nodded. Jasmina smiled and her whole body seemed to relax. Then, once Mrs. Frances had gotten to the *J* names for attendance, Mark turned slightly in his chair to face Mark and raised his eyebrows. Mark responded with a hushed, "Code blue." Mark said, "Me too," and turned back around.

When Mrs. Frances looked back at the *H*s, she saw two boys in matching clothes and one girl in all black, one behind the other, with matching, unsuppressible grins.

Chapter 29

Prime Suspect:
Mark Hopper

When Mark saw a large ant crawling on Pete's binder in computers, he pointed and said as innocently as possible, "There's an ant on your binder."

"Gah!" shouted Pete. He slapped his binder down on a desk. "What's with all these damn ants?"

The computers teacher reprimanded Pete for slamming his binder down and saying "damn," and Pete said, "But there were ants all over my locker this morning!"

Mark stole another glance at the binder, and saw that there were little black dots of dead ants all over it. Inside, he was giving Pete his take-that look.

The computers teacher tried not to smile. "Perhaps you should try to keep your locker more sanitary."

"Yeah, what do you *have* in there that it's infested with bugs?" Mark asked.

"Shut up, Hopper."

"That is *so* disgusting," said one girl to another.

"I know," the girl said back, curling her lip and staring at Pete. "Nasty." The girls giggled.

Pete turned bright red.

"There's an ant on your arm," said Mark.

"Miss Vilansky!" whined Nora Tristam during English. "All these flies are all around Frank, and they're coming onto my desk."

All eyes, including Jonathan's, turned to Frank. Sure enough, there was a swarm of flies circling his head and his desk. A congregation of them seemed to be holding a meeting on the decal on the front of his sweatshirt. He tried to stay still and pretend they weren't there, but after a few seconds he had to try to swat them away.

"Yeah," said the boy who sat in front of Frank. "He's like Pigpen from Charlie Brown."

"You watch Charlie Brown?" Frank said. "What are you, five?"

"Ha!" said a boy in the next row. "He does look like Pigpen!"

Everyone laughed and started to talk. Jonathan included.

Miss Vilansky quieted them down and suggested Frank go freshen up in the restroom.

"If it doesn't work, can he sit somewhere else when he comes back?" Nora asked. "I can't concentrate with all of these flies."

Though Frank and Pete were tormented by the bugs all day, it was Laurie and her locker neighbor who reported the matter to the main office. "My locker couldn't be cleaner," Laurie said. "Someone planted these bugs. It's disgusting."

Ethel called some custodians to clean out their lockers, and a crowd formed—among the crowd were Jasmina and Jonathan—in the hallway as they paraded to the scene with doctor's masks on their faces and buckets full of cleaning products in their hands. Even with the masks concealing their mouths, they seemed disgusted by the dried juice and infestation of mosquitoes. Shortly afterward, the principal, Mr. Haverty, made an announcement over the loudspeaker that anyone with information regarding the "sixth-grade insect incident," or anyone who noticed suspicious behavior that morning or yesterday afternoon, to report to his office immediately. Mark and Mark tried not to look at each other in gym when they heard it, and they both silently prayed that their matching clothing would work according to plan.

It couldn't have worked better.

The boy who had seen Mark at Laurie's locker in the morning when he left the bathroom, anxious to get out of class, went down to the office and reported the suspicious behavior he'd witnessed. "I don't know if it's anything," he said with a shrug, "but I never saw this guy by those lockers before. And it was where the bugs were."

"Do you know who it was?" Mr. Haverty asked.

"I don't know his name," the kid said. "But he was in

khaki pants and a blue collared shirt, tucked in. And he had freckles."

Mr. Haverty mumbled as he wrote it down. "Khaki pants, blue shirt tucked in, freckles. Anything else? Hair color? Eye color?"

"Brown hair. But I have no idea about the eyes. I don't normally gaze into boys' eyes."

Becky Tummelstein also answered the announcement. "I was in school early because my sister got early-morning detention," she explained to Mr. Haverty. "And my mom didn't want to drive here twice. And when I went into the hallway I saw, like, a swarm of flies up by the light."

"Any clue who did it?"

"Well, I did see someone walking away. His back was to me, but it looked like Mark Hopper."

"Mark Hopper . . ." the principal said as though he was trying to wrap the name around his tongue. "What does he look like?"

"Brown hair, freckles, usually wears khaki pants and his shirt tucked in."

"Aha! Just wait here a minute, Miss Tummelstein." Mr. Haverty went across to the main office. "Have you heard of Mark Hopper?" he asked the secretaries.

Their looks said it all. "Which one?" asked one woman.

"There are two?" Mr. Haverty asked.

"Oh yes."

"Then the one with brown hair, freckles, khaki pants, and tucked-in shirt."

"Oh," said Mindy. "*That* Mark Hopper," referring to the one who had stood bug-eyed and scared before her the first day of school.

"Ugh," said Ethel, "*that* Mark Hopper," referring to the Mark Hopper who had marched into the office with a music book and a blue ribbon over the summer.

"Call him down to my office immediately. He's probably responsible for this bug business."

Ethel and Mindy looked at each other. The Mark Hoppers they were thinking of were troublesome, but they weren't troublemakers. "Oh," they both said. "You must mean the *other* Mark Hopper."

"Okay," said the principal, exasperated. "Call the *other* Mark Hopper down immediately, then." He walked back to his own office, where Becky was waiting. "Which Mark Hopper did you see this morning?" he asked her.

Becky cocked her head. "There are two?" she asked.

When Mr. Haverty interrogated Mark Hopper, Mark sat quietly in the large leather chair. His hands were folded neatly in his lap, his ankles were crossed in his khaki pants, and his eyes were wide with fear of the principal. "I had nothing to do with it," he said. "Honest. I'm a good kid. You can ask any of my teachers!" He sighed. "You probably want the other Mark Hopper. I think his sister likes pulling pranks."

When Mr. Haverty interrogated Mark Hopper, Mark sat at the edge of the large leather chair. His arms were crossed angrily in front of his blue collared shirt, and his eyes were fixed on the principal's face. "I had nothing to do with it," he said. "I can't even believe you would accuse me of such a thing. I am a straight-A student. I am above playing stupid pranks. You can ask any of my teachers." He gave him his I-am-sick-of-people-mixing-me-up-with-that-moron look. He rolled his eyes. "You probably want the other Mark Hopper. I think his sister has access to bugs."

After school, Mr. Haverty spoke with a number of Mark's teachers, who all said that Mark was sweet and shy, and they didn't think he was the type to pull pranks. "But doesn't he have a sister who pulled pranks here?" the principal asked.

"I think you're thinking of the other Mark Hopper," they said.

Then he spoke with a number of Mark's teachers, who all said that Mark was outspoken though getting nicer, and they didn't think he was the type to pull pranks.

"But didn't his sister used to pull pranks? Or does she have access to bugs?"

Most of the teachers scratched their heads, and then said politely, "Maybe you're thinking of the other Mark Hopper."

His last hopes were the teachers who had them both in class at the same time. He explained the situation to Mrs. Frances, their homeroom teacher, first. "One has brown hair, and the other has slightly browner hair. But they don't really look alike, see? One is about this tall, and the other's about . . . well, also about this tall. But one of them has a sister who likes bugs, and one of them has a sister who pulled pranks. Or maybe one has both sisters. Or maybe they're the same sister . . . So do you know which one of them might be responsible?"

"I'm not sure, but maybe the one who sits there," Mrs. Frances said slowly, pointing to Mark's seat.

"Okay. Which one is that?"

"He has brown hair," she said, pointing to the principal and nodding. "And freckles, I think."

"So the one with the sister who pulls pranks?"

"Is he the one who usually wears collared shirts?"

"They both do."

"I think the boy I'm thinking of is named . . . Mark Hopper!" declared Mrs. Frances.

Mr. Haverty threw up his hands. "They're both named Mark Hopper!"

Mrs. Frances squinted and rubbed her chin. "You mean there's more than one?" she asked.

The principal gave up.

Chapter 30

Mark Goes to the Tournament

Mark floated on air throughout Thanksgiving weekend. Operation: Bug Dump had gone better than they ever could have hoped, he got an A on a big art project, he got a seventy-eight on a really tough math test, and he and his mom and Beth and Grandpa Murray all flew up to their old town in Massachusetts to spend the long weekend with his dad. Mark spent Friday with Sammy, playing video games and trading comic books and talking about sixth grade. Mark told Sammy all about Jonathan and Jasmina and a lot about the other Mark Geoffrey Hopper, but mostly he talked about Operation: Bug Dump. Beth and Mark begged their dad to tell them what his big surprise was all weekend, and when he refused to budge, they tried to trick him into telling them. They said things like "When's the moving truck arriving, Dad?" And he'd say something mysterious like, "As soon as I call them and arrange it." Mark thought that meant he was all ready to move but hadn't called the truck yet, but Beth warned that it might mean that he didn't yet have a reason to call them. Even so, Mark was so happy all weekend that he returned to Greenburgh feeling like he could conquer just about anything. That Mastermind tournament was in the bag.

Mark also floated on air throughout Thanksgiving weekend. Though he wouldn't admit it to Beth, even he was impressed with how smoothly Operation: Bug Dump had gone. He got a hundred, as usual, on the hardest math test yet, and if Mark's stellar performance on their prank and in the principal's office was any indication of how he'd perform on December 1, he was on his way to Mastermind glory. Even the fact that his dad wasn't there only brought him slightly down. And the fact that when his dad actually called, on Saturday, Mark didn't even get a chance to speak to him, but just jumped up and down and tugged on his mother's shirt until she reminded his dad that the Mastermind awards ceremony was on December 2, only brought him down a little bit more. And the fact that he wished weren't a fact—that after he walked away, content that his mother had reminded his dad about the ceremony, he heard her say "divorce papers"— only made him more sure than ever that Mark's performance the next weekend could make everything better.

On the morning of Saturday, December 1, Mark got ready to go to the tournament as though he were going himself. He put on his crispest pair of khaki pants and his shiniest brown shoes. He tucked in his new collared shirt his mother had purchased for the occasion, and he followed directions from the Internet in order to tie his new tie, since his dad had not shown him how before he left. Looking in the mirror and putting the final touches on his neatly gelled hair, he regretted that he wasn't going to get to show the judges what a Mastermind he was. But then he had a clever thought: I rigged this tournament so that I will win even though I am not even going. Now *that* truly shows I am the cleverest middle schooler in the whole state. Those judges, he reasoned with a smirk at himself in the mirror, wouldn't even know what hit them.

"Oh, look at little Marky Mark going off to his little competition," crooned Beth. She was spread out over the couch in her pajamas. She spit a wad of gum into the air and caught it back in her mouth.

"Have a good day watching baby cartoons," Mark said, "while I am off proving how smart I am."

"Looking sharp!" said his mother. She tousled his perfectly placed hair. Had Mark been planning on actually competing that day, he would have yelled at her and gone back to fix it. But since he wasn't, he just smoothed it with his hand and said, "Let's go. We're going to be late."

There was a large billboard at the entrance to the college where the tournament was taking place. It said WELCOME, STATE-WIDE MASTERMIND FINALISTS! Mrs. Hopper pointed at it and said she wished she had her camera.

"Just bring it tonight when it says, 'Welcome, Mark Hopper, Mastermind Winner,'" Mark said.

"That's the spirit," his mother said. "Do you want me to come in with you to register?"

"No. Just pick me up here at two."

"All right." She reached across the front seat and gave Mark a hug. "Good luck, hon. What do you have to do today?"

"Some teamwork thing and the interview."

"Okay, then. I'll tell you the key to that stuff: just be yourself."

Or in my case, Mark thought as he jumped out of the car, just let someone else be me. He went inside and hid in the bathroom until he was sure his mother had driven away. Then he walked back out and headed down the street to the public library, where he planned on spending the time until his mother picked him up. When he got there, he saw a sign that read PORTRAITS BY IVY ROAD MIDDLE SCHOOL ARTISTS on a wall that was prepped to be adorned with paintings. After the awards ceremony, he would bring the painting here and have the librarians hang it with all of the others that weren't yet up. Everything would go according to plan.

Meanwhile, Mark put on his nicest khakis, which had only one large crease running from the back of the right knee to the back right pocket, and his crispest collared shirt, which was only moderately wrinkled. His mom was working an early-morning shift at the bank, his dad hadn't yet arrived for the weekend, and Grandpa Murray was convinced that Mark needed a ride to Marius College for something related to his surprise birthday present. But Beth and two tree frogs also needed a ride to a classmate's house to work on a tree-frog project. "Why are you dressed already?" Beth asked at breakfast. "Did you forget it's Saturday?"

"Ready to go, kiddos?" Grandpa Murray asked.

"Where do you need to go?" Beth asked Mark.

This was going to be hard. Mark was never dressed before noon on a Saturday, and, more importantly, he never lied to

Beth. He had never kept anything from her, except for once in fourth grade when he told her his teacher hadn't graded their science projects instead of admitting to her that he got a C on his. This was why he had hoped she'd be gone or sleeping when he had to leave. Mark glanced at Grandpa Murray, who raised his hands and said, "I know, I know, I can't listen to this conversation." He left the room.

"What do you have to do involving Grandpa's present?"

"I can't tell you," Mark whispered.

"Why not?" Beth asked, hurt. "I know what the present is."

"I know, but I just can't." Mark looked at her with his large eyes pleading.

Beth crossed her arms. "What are you up to?"

"I just can't tell you. Can you please play along and pretend I have to do something for Grandpa's present? I'll tell you later."

Beth sighed. "Fine. But you'd better not be up to anything that could get you in trouble."

The three of them piled into the car. Mark patted his pants pocket to make sure he had his school ID and Mark's—his—finalist letter. Even though his birthday was tomorrow, Grandpa Murray was still trying harder than ever to find out what his present was. He made guesses all the way to the college. A textbook? An honorary degree? A blind date with a college professor? Both Beth and Mark kept their lips zipped. When they got to the college, Beth looked at Mark in utter bewilderment. Mark shrugged.

"Welcome, Statewide Mastermind Finalists," Grandpa Murray read. "Are you a Statewide Mastermind Finalist?"

"No," Mark said. "Can you pick me up at one-thirty?"

"You bet."

Beth raised one eyebrow. "See you later," she said before they drove off.

Mark waved as they left. He took a deep breath. He felt miserable about lying to his sister and his grandpa. And he had no idea what to expect once he walked through those doors. Maybe I won't even get past registration, he thought hopefully. Then this will all be over.

A boy about his age walked up with what must have been his parents. He was wearing a suit and a clip-on bow tie. "Stand next to the sign, honey," his mother said.

"Yes, right there next to the sign," said his father.

The boy looked at Mark, who was standing next to the sign. "Can you move?" he said.

Mark looked at the sign and his position. "Oh, yeah, sorry."

The boy stood next to the sign and smiled while his father looked through the viewfinder of a minuscule digital camera. "Smile like you've already won!" the mom said. The boy smiled wider, showing off a mouth full of metal.

The father zoomed in and out. "Move a little to the right. No, the right. Oh, okay, your left. But don't stop smiling! Harrison, smile!" The boy—Harrison, Mark figured—shifted and smiled so wide Mark thought his lips might break. The dad was still zooming in and out.

"Dad!" Harrison said through his clenched smile. "Just take it!"

"Well, how can he take it when you're moving your lips?" his mother said. The father zoomed out a bit. "Oh, for goodness' sake, Bob, it focuses automatically."

Mark watched the scene with his eyes so round and absorbed that after the father finally snapped the picture, Harrison looked at him and said, "What are you looking at?"

Mark blinked. "Nothing," he said. The parents ushered Harrison into the building, fussing with his hair and unclipping and reclipping his tie and giving him last-minute practice interview questions. Mark stared after them. He wasn't nearly that prepared. All he had to go on were his background in teamwork games, lessons on talking to adults from the other Mark Hopper, and a rudimentary history of the bassoon. This is an adventure, he reminded himself. It's like I'm in a video game. He remembered the last-minute advice Mark had given him: *Be yourself, and kick everybody else's butt.* He took a deep breath, knocked on the billboard for good luck, and walked in.

"Mastermind tournament?" asked a young woman in a chair just inside. Mark nodded. "Registration is down that hall, turn left." Mark thanked her. This was his first challenge: Level One, Registration.

Two smiley women sat at a desk behind piles of papers, clipboards, record books, and, Mark couldn't help but notice, a basket full of candy. Harrison, who must have just finished checking in, walked into a room nearby, and his parents stood at the door waving.

"Good morning!" one of the women chirped. "Name, please?"

"Mark Geoffrey Hopper," Mark said. He felt his ears go red, even though it wasn't a lie.

"Don't be nervous, Mark," the other woman said. She smiled warmly. "Everyone's a winner who's gotten this far."

Mark gulped.

"Okay," said the first woman. "Mark Geoffrey Hopper. Well,

you didn't have to travel far this morning! Some people had to take a plane or drive a few hours, but you're from right here in Greenburgh! I just need your school ID and your finalist letter."

This was it. The moment of truth. Mark reached into his pocket and handed them both over. While the second woman flipped through a pile of large name tags, the first glanced at his ID and his letter and handed them back. Mark couldn't believe it. She barely even looked at his ID! He could have given her his library card instead, or his Buy Five Doughnuts Get One Free card. This was too easy.

"Here is your name tag, Mark. It's kind of big, I know, but just put it around your neck so the judges and the other Masterminds will know who you are. And then you're all set!"

Mark put the name tag, which was the size of a piece of loose-leaf paper and in a flimsy plastic sleeve, around his neck and his ID and finalist letter back into his pocket. "That's it?" he asked.

"That's it," one of the women said with a friendly chuckle. "Go into this room right here. You can get to know the other finalists for a bit. The judges will explain everything else in about ten minutes when they're ready to start. You can take some candy if you'd like." She pointed to the basket. "Help yourself."

"Good luck!" the other added.

"Thank you!" Mark said brightly. He scooped a whole handful of fun-size chocolate bars and individually wrapped mini licorice sticks. He couldn't wait to tell Mark that they hadn't even really looked at his ID. Why had he been nervous at all? If that was the kind of security they had for this tournament, they were almost asking for people to send other people with their names in their place.

He walked into the room to find about ten competitors sitting in a circle of chairs with desks attached, just like the ones at Ivy Road Middle School. They all looked slightly older, were dressed fancier, and were visibly nervous. None of them were talking, and only one of them was eating candy. Mark took an empty seat between a chubby Asian girl with circular glasses who was wearing a fluffy pink dress and a skinny girl with a ponytail of curly hair wearing black pants and a yellow sweater. Mark smoothed his shirt. "Hi," he said. "I'm Mark." He dropped his handful of candy on his desk and began to open one of the Twizzlers. He glanced around and pointed to his stash. "Would anyone like some?"

The Asian girl, whose name tag said Grace, didn't even look at him. The curly-haired one smiled and asked, "Really?" When Mark nodded vigorously, she stuck out her hand and grabbed a couple chocolate bars. "Thanks. I'm Emily," she said. "What grade are you in?"

That's a weird question, Mark thought. Isn't this the sixth-grade part of the competition? "Sixth," he said.

"Sixth!" said Emily. Almost all of the others in the room looked at him, too. Some looked impressed, while others looked resentful. Harrison got up, walked to Mark's desk, and took a peanut-butter cup. Grace snorted but still stared straight ahead. "Wow," said Emily.

"Why, what grade are you in?" Mark asked innocently.

"Seventh," she said. That showed how much Mark knew. Apparently everyone in middle school was lumped together to compete.

"I'm seventh," said someone else.

"Who else is seventh?" Harrison asked the group. No one responded. "Eighth?" Harrison asked. Everyone but Mark, Emily, the other seventh grader, and Grace raised their hands. "You're in sixth then, too?" Harrison asked Grace.

"That's my business, not yours," Grace snapped.

Mark laughed to himself. Mark might have come as himself after all. He and Grace would make a great pair. "So no one else is in sixth?" he said. "Except maybe you," he said with a nod to Grace.

Everybody but Grace giggled and shook their heads. It must be nearly impossible to become a finalist in sixth grade, Mark realized. He suddenly had a newfound respect for Mark. He beat out a lot of older kids for Mark to be here, like Mark had done by being the only sixth grader whose painting was going to be in the library. On the one hand, he had a lot to live up to. On the other, if he didn't win it wouldn't be a big deal—to anyone but Mark, at least—because nobody would expect him to—except Mark.

A *clack-clack-clack* noise announced the entrance of a tall, wiry woman with pepper-colored hair and rimless glasses. She was wearing a cranberry-colored wool skirt and matching suit jacket. The clacking was made by her cranberry-colored heels on the hard floor, and it didn't stop when she reached the room, for she tapped her foot while standing outside the circle of competitors and reviewing the contents of a clipboard. "Good morning," she said severely. Mark wasn't sure if he should say "good morning" back, so he was glad when she continued without waiting for a return greeting. "I am Dr. Latchky, and I will be running the competition today. I'd like to thank you all for coming and congratulate you on getting this far. The other judges are on their way, and we will begin shortly, first with the teamwork component and then, after that, lunch and the interviews. Are there any questions at this point?"

No one had any. As quietly as he could, Mark brushed his candy into a pile and transferred it under his desk. He finished his Twizzler and stuck the wrapper in his pocket. Three other adults entered the room one after another. The first were a woman and a man who were dressed similarly to Dr. Latchky and looked friendly enough, if not warm and welcoming. The last was a man so short and squat he had to squeeze through the door sideways. He was wearing a suit and clack-clacking shoes like the others, but his face was drenched in sweat that he wiped occasionally with a light blue handkerchief. As he waddled into the classroom and toward his post in a corner, he was grinning from ear to ear. "Good morning!" he said cheerily to the group. This time Mark and a few others said "good morning" back.

Mark caught him eyeing his candy beneath the desk. He looked down at the candy and back up with eyes as wide as the man he faced. "Would you like some?" he asked.

The judge bounced as he laughed. "Thank you, young man," he said. "Don't mind if I do." He started to bend down, but Mark leaned down first and came up with a Twizzler. "Perfect," the man said. "Perfect!"

Mark liked him. He just hoped he didn't play the bassoon.

After the judges and the students introduced themselves, the games began. Their first task—a warm-up, the judges called it—was to count aloud, with individuals calling out a number at a time starting with one, until they got to fifteen. If two people spoke at the same time, they would have to start back at one. Mark had never tried this before, but it sounded easy.

"Begin whenever you're ready," Dr. Latchky said.

The group sat in silence for a few seconds, everyone looking at one another. Then Grace and Harrison announced at the same time, "One!"

Mark and some others laughed, including the hefty judge, who had introduced himself as Professor Clugg. They fell into silence again.

"One!" said Grace, who was speaking a few octaves higher and a few notches sweeter now that there were judges in the room.

"Two," said Harrison and another boy at the same time.

Grace, frustrated, said, "One" again immediately, but another girl had had the same idea.

Then the room became quiet once more. "One," said Emily slowly.

"Two," Mark said. He stared at Grace with his eyes wide. If they went in order around the circle, this would be a piece of cake. He figured Professor Clugg liked cake.

She picked up on the idea and said, "Three," but not before a boy across the circle had already started saying it, too. Grace glared at him. Then, in case the judges had noticed, she glanced at them at smiled.

Emily began again with one, and Mark took two, then Grace three. They made it without a mistake until they were almost back at Emily, when someone who wasn't paying close attention said ten instead of nine. But Emily started up with one again, and they made it around without a problem. "All right!" whooped Mark after they reached fifteen. "That was great!" Emily gave him a high five and a couple others clapped their hands, including Professor Clugg. Grace sat looking smug, as though the number seven had single-handedly bought them the victory.

Dr. Latchky congratulated them, but told them to try it once more, this time without having a specific order. That was much harder, but now that they were all in the spirit of the game and up to the challenge, they did it without too much trouble and without any two people shouting out "one" at the same time; it was as though they had a sort of unspoken communication about who was going to go next. After a few tries, two girls said "fifteen" at the same time, and everybody laughed and sighed, but the next time they succeeded without a hitch. Mark unwrapped a Hershey's Kiss and popped it into his mouth. He almost completely forgot that he was not supposed to be there.

The next game was a teamwork classic: the human knot. From the expressions on his competitors' faces, Mark could tell that many of them knew it, too. They pushed the desks to the walls and stood in a circle in the center, then joined hands with people across the circle, creating an enormous web of arms. The challenge was to untangle themselves without releasing their hands. This had been challenging when Mark played it in gym class. But that was nothing compared to playing it with a group of young Masterminds. Everyone had a solution, and everyone wanted theirs to be the one that worked.

"You go under there first," said Grace, pointing with her chin.

"No," said the girl she had directed. "I think you—um, Harrison, right?—you need to slide your hand lower and step over that arm."

"That's not a good way to start, though," said Harrison. "Why don't we each just get ourselves in comfortable positions first?"

"I like that idea," said Emily, whose arms were stretched

like opposite ends of a tug-of-war rope in the wrong directions.

"But really," Grace said. "That's not going to help unless *she* goes under there first. Don't you see why?"

"I can't see anything," said a boy who was bent over to the left in order to keep holding on to Mark's hand.

"Let's do Harrison's idea," said Emily.

"I'm telling you, it's not going to wo-orrk," Grace sang.

"Who ca-ares?" sang someone else in the same tone. "We can always come back. I've done this before."

The judges exchanged knowing looks and took careful notes on their clipboards.

"I've done this before, too, for your information."

"Me too, but it doesn't matter. We need to start doing *something*."

"So are we doing my idea?" Harrison asked with a glance toward Dr. Latchky.

"I'm going under here, okay?"

"And I'm going to step over your hand."

"Ouch!"

"I told you I was going under!"

"I didn't know you were talking to me! I wasn't ready."

One of the judges sighed.

"You guys," said Mark. "We need to work *together*."

"Why don't we pick someone's plan and try it? I say Harrison's plan."

"What was Harrison's plan?"

"My plan," Harrison announced, "is to first have everyone get comfortable so that we can think and see straight."

"Good idea," said Mark, who was crouched below the center of the knot and couldn't see anything except Professor Clugg, who had bent over and reached for a piece of candy. Mark just wanted to stop arguing and start untangling.

But they carried on in this way for another five minutes. They barely got halfway free, and the judges kept writing long after Dr. Latchky asked them to return to their seats. That was an utter failure, Mark knew, but at least it was an utter failure for everyone. If Mark was there, he probably would have made sure everyone knew that if they had tried his idea, they would have gotten out.

After one last teamwork game, a man came into the room rolling a large cart full of food. Neither Mark nor Professor Clugg could help but stare wide-eyed as he began arranging the spread on a table: sandwiches, chicken nuggets, soft drinks, and brownies. Mark said "thank you!" with such fervor that everyone else rushed to thank him as well, with Grace being the loudest. The judges left the room to confer and give the competitors time to eat, and Mark piled his plate high with some of everything. It was worth being there just for the food! He was finishing his second brownie when Dr. Latchky came in with her clipboard hugged close to her.

"We are now going to begin with the interviews. Please stay here until you are called. After you're called, you may go, and we will see you all at the awards ceremony tomorrow. The first up is Grace Chen. Next up will be Mark Hopper. Grace, come along with me when you are ready."

Grace threw away the remains of her lunch and smoothed her pink dress. She picked up a large binder overflowing with certificates and report cards before strutting out of the room after Dr. Latchky, stopping in the doorway to fluff up of the bottom of the skirt. "Good luck!" shouted Mark.

With the interviews officially starting, everyone became more nervous. A few competitors who had still been munching on lunch pushed their food aside, no longer hungry. Harrison went into a corner and closed his eyes and mumbled to himself, looking serious but smiling every once in a while. Emily got up and started pacing. Mark sat still, absentmindedly sipping his root beer. The morning was so much fun that he wasn't really worried about the interview. Dr. Latchky and the others were intimidating, but Professor Clugg was nothing but funny. Something about him reminded Mark of Grandpa Murray— though the professor was half Grandpa's age and three times his weight—and there was nothing nerve-racking about talking to Grandpa Murray. He remembered that Mark had said the finalists' art would probably be on display somewhere nearby. He was very curious to see everyone's artwork, especially Mark's. Mark probably submitted a self-portrait, Mark figured. A self-portrait of himself with wings and a halo made of lots of letter *A*s. He laughed out loud at the mental picture, but everyone was too busy preparing him or herself for the final stage of the competition to even look at him. Mark considered slipping out to find the artwork, but since he was next and he didn't want to be missing when he was called, he decided to wait until after his interview.

After about twenty minutes, Grace strutted back in looking perfectly smug. She kept her nose up as she gathered her coat and purse, which Mark assumed she left in the room purposely so that she could come back after her interview and show everyone how confident she looked. Dr. Latchky called Mark's name and told the next finalist to get ready. Amazingly, Mark wasn't nervous at all. All he had to do was be Mark Geoffrey Hopper.

Dr. Latchky led Mark out of the room and down the hall to another, larger room, where the other judges were sitting be-hind a long table. She motioned to a single chair opposite the panel. Mark gulped as he sat down. Professor Clugg also gulped, as he was finishing off a doughnut. Mark laughed. He really did like Professor Clugg.

"Welcome, Mark," said Dr. Latchky. "Good job this morning."

Mark's ears turned red. "Thank you," he said shyly.

"How was lunch?" Professor Clugg asked.

Mark's eyes brightened. He grinned. "Lunch was awesome! Thank you!"

The judges laughed. "You're very welcome," one of them said.

One of the registration women knocked gently on the door and poked her head in. "Sorry to interrupt," she said, "but I've got the painting."

"Ah, yes," said Dr. Latchky. "That's great. Bring it in."

Chapter **31**

Mark's Painting

The woman smiled and opened the door wider. She carried in a wooden easel and set it up at the edge of the judges' panel, facing Mark. Then she carried in a canvas the size of Mark's portrait of Grandpa Murray and placed it on the easel. She spent a few seconds positioning it, then stepped back to admire it for a second. It wasn't until she walked away that Mark could see what the painting was. The woman smiled at Mark and crossed her fingers to wish him luck before she left, but Mark was too busy staring at the painting to notice. His eyes were as round as the doughnut Professor Clugg had just finished. It was his painting. It was his portrait of Grandpa Murray.

"Why is this here?" Mark asked.

"Don't worry," said Dr. Latchky. "After your interview we'll return it to room 104 to display with all of the others."

194

"But—" Mark tried to wrap his tongue around the words he wanted. But first he had to wrap his brain around what was going on. "But, how . . . how did this painting—this portrait of my grandpa—how did it *get* here?"

The judges looked at one another with arched brows. Professor Clugg spoke up. "Well, we brought all of the finalists' artistic pieces over here from our headquarters in Baltimore. After you sent it in with your application, that is." He raised his finger in a sort of semi-understanding. "This *was* your submission of artistic talent, right?"

Dr. Latchky flipped pages on her clipboard. "Yes," she said. "Mark Geoffrey Hopper. Painted portrait of old man and CD with bassoon solo." She looked at the painting and squinted. "Your name is on it," she said. "Did you forget that this is the piece you chose to submit? It was quite some time ago."

Mark's eyes became even wider as he put the pieces together. So the other Mark had submitted this with his name on it. He had sent it in as evidence of his own artistic talent. Without telling him. How had he managed that? Did he steal it from the art room when no one was looking? Or did he just walk in and say he was Mark Geoffrey Hopper and he needed his painting? Mark felt his breathing becoming heavier and his mouth becoming tighter. How could Mark do this to him? He knew how hard he'd worked on that painting, how proud he was that it was going to be the only portrait by a sixth grader to hang in the public library. How was it possibly going to be in the library tomorrow if it was here right now? His stomach, full of chocolate and chicken and root beer, began to churn and tighten. However Mark had done it, he had done it "quite some time ago." And then he had just continued to become Mark's friend, pretending like there wasn't a lie between them the size of . . . of . . . the size of Professor Clugg! And here was Mark doing him a favor and cheating for him. Mark was right, he was an idiot.

Here was his chance to give his namesake what he deserved. He would confess to the judges that "he" had stolen the painting, and then Mark would be disqualified.

The judges wrinkled their foreheads and rechecked their records. They looked at one another and at Mark, concerned. "Do you want to take a few minutes to relax, and we'll interview Benjamin first?" Dr. Latchky asked.

Mark shifted his gaze from the painting to the judges. So Mark wanted to win this competition *this* badly, he thought. So badly he'd cheat *twice* and risk losing one of two people he could actually call a friend? He knew he should feel angry. Furious. But instead he just felt sad. Gut-wrenchingly, heart-crumblingly sad.

He shook his head. "I'm sorry," he said to the judges. He spoke as confidently as he could, directing his words mostly at Professor Clugg and remembering everything Mark had taught him about projection and authority. "I just, um, panicked a little because I *did* forget that I submitted that painting. And it's supposed to be hung in the library tomorrow so I can show it to my grandpa as a surprise birthday present, and I'm worried now that it can't be."

"Oh," said Dr. Latchky, looking extremely relieved. "Well, we only need it for the rest of the day, so I'm sure it can all be worked out. You can take it home after the awards ceremony tonight and to the library in the morning. Are you all right to continue on with the interview, then?"

Mark nodded. He was ready.

Chapter 32

Mark's Confrontation

It was only 12:50 when Mark was finished interviewing and ready to leave, and Grandpa Murray wasn't going to arrive until 1:30. By the time Mark walked to the public library and found an antsy-looking Mark in the reference section flipping through a book called *The 50 Greatest Minds of the Twentieth Century*, it was just after one o'clock.

This morning in the library had felt like the longest three hours of Mark's life. He toured aisle after aisle and opened book after book, but no matter the book, he just couldn't seem to keep his mind on it. He thought constantly about how the competition was going. From ten until eleven he had worried that Mark had overslept, or he'd not been able to get his grandpa to drive him, or he'd gotten lost on the way and got there too late to register. He worried that they would quiz him on his address and birthday on his way in, and that they'd be found out right away. But eleven had come and gone—slowly but without word, so from eleven until twelve he wondered if Mark was doing well in the teamwork portion, or if the task they gave them was something really tough and mathematical, and he should have gone himself. He wondered what the other finalists were like, and how many of them were sixth graders. And from twelve until one he worried about the interviews. Would Mark just sit there staring at the panel of judges like they were ghosts? Or would he speak so softly and hesitantly they wouldn't hear him? All of these thoughts were interspersed with fantasies about reuniting with his dad, for good, at the awards ceremony. He pictured his dad's face glowing with pride, and his mother and sister melting at the sight and deciding to become a proper family again. He couldn't *stand* waiting.

So when he looked up from *The 50 Greatest Minds of the Twentieth Century* and saw Mark sitting next to him, he nearly choked on his own excitement. "You're done early! I thought I wouldn't talk to you until later. That was really smart of you to come here. How'd it go? Tell me everything, but mostly the important parts." Mark just stared at him, but not with any readable emotion. It made Mark even more nervous. He said, "Come on. What happened? Was it really bad? How was the teamwork thing? Was it stupid?"

A librarian shushed Mark sternly. "Let's go outside," Mark whispered. "You probably shouldn't tell me anything in here where people can hear anyway." He hurriedly put on his coat and gloves and led Mark into a small vestibule near the back door of the library. Once they were there he pressed him again. "Say something, for pete's sake. Even if it went really badly, just tell me—I can take it," he lied. "How was the teamwork part?"

"The teamwork part was fine. I think I did pretty well."

"Great! And the interview?"

"The interview went fine for the most part. I used all the techniques we went over, about speaking loudly and clearly, and making eye contact, and I wasn't nervous."

"Okay. But it was only okay for the most part? Did they ask you what you think the most important middle school skill is?"

"Yes," said Mark.

"I knew it. Did you give the answer we planned?"

"Yes."

"What else? What else did they ask you? Did they ask about the bassoon at all?"

"Not much about the bassoon; more about art."

"Perfect!" Mark clapped his hands. "You know a lot about art."

"Yeah," Mark said. "And they asked a lot about the painting that you submitted." He looked Mark square in the eye, just the way he had taught him to.

Mark froze. He tried to look casual. "Oh, they asked you about it?"

"They had it there," Mark said. "In the room."

Neither of them spoke for a whole minute. An old woman walked between them in the vestibule to leave. Then Mark spoke again. "I just don't get it. How come you stole it? You knew it was my grandpa's birthday present, and that I wanted it to go in the library."

"You weren't ever going to find out," Mark said. "I was going to bring it to the library on time—"

"I lied to my grandpa for you, and I lied to my sister, all because I thought we were friends. And you were just lying to me."

"Listen," Mark said. "I did that a long time ago, before we were friends. And it's not like I felt good about it."

"*Before* we were friends?" Mark asked. "Meaning right now we are friends?"

"Yes," Mark said. "I mean, I hope so."

"I don't believe you. I think you were just using me to help you cheat. You just pretended to be nice because we have the same name. You probably had this planned all along."

"No, I didn't."

"Yeah, right. You pretended to be nice to me so that you could learn all about my painting, and then you pretended to be nice so that you could convince me to go in your place today."

"No, I wasn't just pretending."

"Yes, you were. You were faking it. And you know what?" Mark stiffened. He found the anger that had been blocked by sadness during his interview. And he found the words to express it. "You aren't very good at being nice, even when you're faking it!"

"Shut up!" snapped Mark reflexively. "I told you, I wasn't faking it, and I wasn't planning it all along. I took the painting when I still hated you and thought you were ruining my life."

"When you *hated* me?"

"Yes."

"Well, I hated you, too! And I should have never stopped hating you! All you care about is being the best, but if you're really the best, how come you couldn't even win this dumb competition without my help?"

"It is not a dumb competition," Mark growled.

"Yes it is! You just don't think it is because it's all you have.

Maybe if you actually knew how to be a normal person, you wouldn't have to care so much about winning stupid contests, because people would actually like you."

"Oh yeah? You're just jealous because you couldn't win anything that requires an ounce of brains. You would be flunking the sixth grade if I wasn't wasting all of my time helping you!"

"You'd be the most hated person in the whole town if some people didn't think you were me!"

"And you'd be in all the stupid-kid classes if you hadn't accidentally gotten *my* class schedule!"

Mark stopped. Was that true? Was he only in honors classes because he had gotten Mark's schedule? He remembered his surprise and delight when he saw his schedule that day in August, before he knew of the other Mark Geoffrey Hopper or anyone else in Greenburgh. Of course he didn't deserve to be in advanced classes. Why hadn't he realized that until Mark said it just now? He really was stupid. He really couldn't figure out anything without Mark's help. He felt completely deflated, like a shriveled-up balloon. He turned around before Mark could see his round eyes well up with tears, muttering something about needing to get back to get picked up.

"Hey," Mark said. His voice quivered. He did only have the contest, especially now that Mark hated him. Mark would tell Jasmina and Jonathan and he'd lose his last microscopic speck of friendship. Who was he even kidding when he thought he could make and keep a friend? He couldn't even keep his own dad. Mark was right—he needed the stupid contest more than ever. "So you told them the truth? Are we in really big trouble?"

"Go to the awards ceremony and see," Mark said quietly.

"You didn't tell?"

Mark shrugged.

"So I—we—could still win?"

Mark faced Mark and crossed his arms. "What is *wrong* with you?"

"It's just . . . I just . . ." He swallowed. He closed his eyes. "I need to win to bring my dad back." He opened his eyes back up and looked at Mark. "You understand—because your dad left, too."

"Left? My dad just couldn't move here with us until he got a new job and sold our old house. I think he's moving back this weekend. What do you mean *left*? And why would winning a competition bring someone back?"

Mark felt lied to and cheated, raw and exposed. His breath came heavy and furious, and his eyes were hot. Looking at Mark—this Mark whose dad was moving back this weekend—made him furious. He threw down his gloves and lunged at Mark, pushing him up against the building. Mark pushed him back, and it wasn't long before two boys who had never thrown a punch before in their lives had given each other matching black eyes.

Chapter **33**

Mark's Confrontation

"What happened to you?" Mrs. Hopper demanded.

Mark flipped down the passenger seat's sun visor and looked in the mirror. His right eye was swollen into a squint with a bluish half-moon underneath it. His head was throbbing and his nose was still a little bloody, but he somehow felt the best he had in months.

"What happened?" Mrs. Hopper repeated. She put the car in park and refused to drive until Mark answered. "What were you doing in there, Mark?"

"I was at the tournament," Mark said.

"Mark Geoffrey Hopper, people do not fistfight at the state-wide Mastermind finals. Especially you. Did you provoke someone? Did he attack you? If you won't talk, I'll take you to the police station."

"I think I really might win," Mark said cheerfully. "We need to go to the awards ceremony tonight."

"That isn't funny, Mark. Get out my cell phone from my purse beneath your seat. I'm going to call your sister and tell her I can't bring her to the mall because I'm taking you to the police station."

Mark reached into his mother's bag and found her phone. He began to scroll through the phone numbers she had stored in there.

"That is private, Mark. Hand it to me. Mark, *now*."

But Mark had stopped in the *C*s. "Chuck." He clicked on the entry to view the number. It was a local area code. His father had a phone number with a local area code, and his mother not only knew that he had it, but had it stored in her phone. Yet she had never told him so that he could call him whenever he wanted to instead of waiting weeks, sometimes months, until he had almost given up hope that he would pick up their house phone and hear his dad's voice on the other end. "How many people named Chuck do you know?" Mark asked.

His mother's silence answered for her.

"Why didn't you tell me that you knew Dad's phone number?"

His mother sighed and slowly lowered her forehead to the steering wheel.

"Mom! Why didn't you tell me?" Mark demanded. When she didn't answer, he pressed send.

"Mark, please, honey . . ."

Mark held the phone up to his ear. It was ringing. After three rings someone picked up. "Chuck Hopper," said his father.

"Dad!" said Mark. "It's me, Mark."

His mother sighed and looked out the window, her expression vaguely hopeful.

Mr. Hopper sounded surprised, which didn't surprise Mark. "Oh, hi, Mark. How did you get this number?"

"Mom's phone. Dad, I think I won the Mastermind tournament! It was today and it went really well, and I am practically one hundred percent sure that I won. So I'll see you at the awards ceremony tonight? It's at eight o'clock at Marius College, right in Greenburgh."

"Oh, that's great, bud—"

"I know! You won that tournament every year in middle school. I'll get a trophy that matches yours, and then next year I'll get another one, and then the next year I'll get a third."

"That's the Hopper way. But listen, Mark, I'm really very busy right now."

"I know, so I'll just see you at the awards ceremony. Tonight."

"Mark, I don't know if I'm going to be able to make it."

"There'll be newspaper reporters there and stuff—"

"Mark, I need to go."

"You said you'd come. It shouldn't go for very long."

"It doesn't matter," Mr. Hopper snapped. "I can't come. I'm out of town."

Mark heard something in the background. It sounded like a woman laughing. His head started to throb and his black eye began to twitch. "Okay, well, that's okay. When will you be back? You can come home and see the trophy. I'm going to display it right where you kept yours."

"Yeah, I'll try," Mr. Hopper said.

Mark's heart stung. That was what he had said about the awards ceremony.

"Tell your mother to have her lawyer give mine the papers. She'll know what I mean."

Of course she would, Mark thought. It didn't take a genius to know that that meant divorce papers. He reached his hand up to his face and felt his black eye. He thought about what Mark had said before he pushed him: *Why would winning a competition bring someone back?* Why would it? Why would anyone even think that it would? What would that trophy do except remind him how he could win at everything except things that matter?

His mother was looking at him with a sad smile. He muttered a good-bye into the phone and pressed end. He reached over with the intention of handing the phone to his mother, but found himself hugging her tightly instead.

Chapter 34

Mark Hopper:
Master Thief

Grandpa Murray opened the door to find Mark on the stoop—side-parted hair, gravelly freckles, black eye and all. His bicycle was in the driveway with a helmet dangling from one of the handlebars. "Can I help you?" Grandpa Murray asked.

"Is Mark home?"

"Are you the one who socked him?"

Mark nodded slowly. "Did he tell you?"

"Nah, he's no snitch. Lucky guess. Did you come to apologize?"

Mark nodded again.

"Who won, then?"

Mark tried not to smile. "Mark Hopper," he said.

Grandpa Murray laughed heartily. "Good answer. Mark's

not home. All the Hoppers went out and left me here to stand guard in case Mark's attacker figured out where he lives."

"What are you supposed to do now that I'm here?"

Grandpa Murray shrugged. "You know, I don't know. Do you want to come inside? It looks like you've had a rough day."

Mark thought. He had something he needed to accomplish, and it would be ten times easier to do with a car rather than a bicycle. And if he was going to get a ride, it had to be from someone who didn't ask questions. "I know I really don't deserve any favors, but do you think you can help me with something? It's something I owe Mark."

"It's not another punch in the nose, is it?"

"No, sir."

"What do you need?"

On the drive to the college, Grandpa Murray kept perfectly silent. Maybe it was because he didn't ask, or maybe it was because Mark had told Mark that Grandpa Murray was good at forgetting things you wanted him to forget, or maybe it was just because Mark needed to talk. Whatever the reason, he started telling Grandpa Murray what had happened to him that afternoon. He told him about the phone call to his dad, and about how his plan to win him back had not just failed miserably, but caused him countless other miserable failures. "Why," Mark asked, his voice shaking, "why would someone leave his family?"

"Because he's stupid," Grandpa Murray said.

Mark's eyes widened.

"If some turkey leaves his family," Grandpa Murray continued, "it's because it's him who has a problem—not any of his family members. And a turncoat like that needs to figure it out for himself. Sometimes they do and sometimes they don't. But it's not worth trying to catch someone who's not ready to be caught. You're better off just being thankful for what you've got." He paused. "That's why I never try to look for underwear I leave behind somewhere in the house after I shower. I'm just grateful to have a fresh pair of underwear to put on, or at least a dirty one I can turn inside out until I do some laundry. That's always been my approach. And that's why my daughter finds me so impossible and my grandchildren find me so funny." He paused. "Why was I talking about underwear?"

Mark smiled. "Park right here," he said. "I'm going to go in and get something . . . but it's something you're not supposed to see yet."

"I'll close my eyes."

"Not while you're driving! Just . . . if you do see something, you have to pretend tomorrow that you're seeing it for the first time."

"You got it."

Mark jumped out and walked as confidently into the college as he had into the art wing a few weeks ago. The only trouble was he didn't know where to look this time. He walked down a long hallway and peeked in every room, but he didn't see anything. Turning the corner, he saw a table with a sign that said MASTERMIND hanging off it, but the table itself was empty and there wasn't anyone in sight. He looked into the room right by the table, but there wasn't any artwork in there. He heard a door opening and voices flowing out into the hallway. "I'm pleased with our choice," a woman said. He ducked into the open room and pressed his back up against the wall. Shoes clacked on the hard floor as the people passed, still chatting. "Yes," a man's voice said. "He was my first choice from the start."

The footsteps approached the room where Mark was, and scooted behind the door and held his breath. "Where'd the artwork go?" a woman's voice asked.

"Oh," another woman responded. "They must have already brought it all into the auditorium for tonight."

"That was quick," the first voice said.

"Nah, it's been a few hours since all the kids left."

"It has, hasn't it? That teamwork thing made the day fly by."

The voices and footsteps moved away from the room until Mark couldn't hear them anymore. He slipped out of the room and walked as calmly as he could toward the auditorium, remembering the map of the building that had come with his finalist information packet. He opened a door and found himself on the auditorium stage, staring into a sea of empty seats. For a brief moment, he allowed himself to pretend all of those seats were full—the first few rows with press—and that he was up there being handed a trophy. He wondered if he and Mark really were going to win. He spotted Mark's painting across the stage. It was at the end of a line of other artwork, center stage. It was by far the best of them all. He took it and carried it proudly out to the car.

Grandpa Murray covered his eyes while Mark placed it carefully in the backseat. Mark came back up front and they drove down to the library. Grandpa Murray covered his eyes again when Mark jumped out, took the painting, and closed both doors. When Mark left, Grandpa Murray was bursting with pride. The birthday present was so good, he thought he was looking at himself in the rearview mirror.

Mark carried the painting to the hallway where it was to be hung. A few librarians and Mark's art teacher were arranging other paintings on the wall. Mark slipped Mark's portrait into the hall while they fussed over the placement of a picture of a woman with a guitar. He then hid behind a stack of books, crossing his fingers and waiting for them to discover it without him having to reveal himself. They did.

"Here!" shouted the art teacher. "This is the portrait that was missing from the bunch! Oh my, I am *so* glad I don't have to tell Mark that I lost it. Look! Look! Isn't it just wonderful? A sixth grader painted this of his grandfather. He's just about the nicest boy in the world, too. Mark Hopper."

Chapter **35**

Trouble at the
Awards Ceremony

The Mastermind finalists sat in a line in the front row of the college auditorium, clothes ironed, shoes shined, and teeth brushed. They said little to one another, except maybe a muffled "hi" or a fingers-crossed "good luck." Grace had gotten there early and secured the seat at the aisle, since she wanted quick and graceful access to the stage when her name was called to accept the award. Harrison's parents fussed over him until he told them, through gritted teeth, to please go sit down in the back. There were twelve seats with "Reserved for Mastermind Finalists" signs masking-taped to them, but only eleven of them were occupied.

The committee sat on the left end of the stage in a line, Dr. Latchky looking prim in a fresh suit and Professor Clugg looking almost dapper with his large tummy tucked into a brown suit and a navy bow tie stretched around his large neck. At the end of the line of judges was Congresswoman Judy Shane, a petite woman with a big wave of hair above her bangs. To her left was the large Mastermind trophy, and eleven minds (and almost as many pairs of eyes) in the front row were fixed on it.

The judges' minds, however, were focused on the artwork at the other end of the stage. There was a line of familiar paintings, drawings, and one sculpture, but at the end of it, closest to center stage, was an empty space. Dr. Latchky had noticed an empty easel when she arrived for the ceremony a half hour earlier. Figuring out which painting was missing immediately— she could practically sense its absence—she began frantically searching the surrounding area. When the other judges and the tournament assistants arrived, she had them split up to join her in scouring the building. But it wasn't anywhere to be found, even in the cafeteria, which Professor Clugg searched scrupulously. It was extremely troubling. They had all fallen in love with that painting and the old man in it from the start—it was the rich, sweet icing that topped off an otherwise flawless competition entry—but it seemed to be the source of endless trouble today. First its artist, who had done so well in the teamwork games, nearly collapsed when he saw it. And now there seemed to be no answer but that it had been stolen. Dr. Latchky made sure the empty easel was cleared away so that it wouldn't be obvious that one of the paintings had gone missing, but she was sure that Mark Hopper and his family would spot its absence right away and barrage her with questions. She dreaded having to tell them that that brilliant piece of art was gone. But now that she looked out into the front row, where all of the children she had interviewed and observed that afternoon were anxiously awaiting the results of their efforts, she saw that Mark Hopper himself was missing. Dr. Latchky didn't like trouble. She hoped both Mark Hopper and his painting would appear before the night was over, and that no explanations would be necessary, except maybe to her from whoever had taken it. Throughout her welcoming remarks and introduction of Congresswoman Judy Shane, Dr. Latchky kept glancing into the darkness, hoping to make out the figure of a skinny, freckled boy with a canvas in his arms making his way to the front row.

But neither boy nor painting had arrived when Judy Shane concluded her speech, and it was time for the announcement of the winners. The congresswoman took an envelope from the pocket of her suit and placed it on the podium. "You are all unbelievable students and individuals," she began. "The judges informed me that this group made it extremely difficult to choose a winner. So before I continue, I'd like everyone here to give these twelve fine young men and women a round of applause."

Everyone did, but the students barely heard it. They were focusing on Congresswoman Shane, who had opened the envelope.

"I will first announce the two runners-up. For outstanding applications all around, impressive teamwork abilities, and warm brilliance in their interviews, I'd like to present runners-up certificates to . . . Harrison Naylor and Emily Wolen!"

The audience cheered and cheered while Harrison and Emily walked to the stage, shook Mrs. Shane's hand, and accepted their certificates. All of the seated finalists sat up straighter. Mark's seat remained empty.

"And now, for the presentation of this big trophy. This year's Mastermind winner blew away the judges before they even met him. He has a stellar academic record, a strong voice and command of words, which was evident in his essay, and a gift for music—he plays the bassoon. Among his many talents is advanced skill at painting; he took the committee's breath away with a painted portrait entitled *Grandpa*." She pointed behind her, not realizing that there was no *Grandpa* to point out. "Yet despite all of this, our Mastermind winner remains a down-to-earth team player and modest, genuine young man. It has been a long time since someone in the sixth grade has won the Mastermind trophy. But it is my honor and pleasure to present this year's Mastermind trophy to Mark Geoffrey Hopper."

The audience applauded, but no one came up to accept the trophy. After almost a minute, everyone began to look around. "Mark Hopper," repeated Judy Shane. She looked back at the judges behind her. The room buzzed. Where was Mark Hopper?

"Well," said Judy Shane after a moment. She looked incredibly uneasy. "It seems like Mark Hopper was unable to be here tonight."

Everyone murmured louder. A woman tiptoed onto the stage from the wings and whispered in the congresswoman's ear. "I have just been informed that there is someone here who can accept the trophy on Mark's behalf and deliver it to him along with our congratulations. Mr. Doug Haverty? Principal of Ivy Road Middle School?"

Sure enough, Mr. Haverty was sitting in the center of the auditorium. He had received a call from someone from the committee informing him that one of his students was going to be named the winner. He had been proud of Mark, of course, and wanted to come to congratulate him, but he also was still hoping to get to the bottom of the bug business. Surely the Mark Hopper who would walk up onstage tonight would not be the Mark Hopper he had tried to catch last week. But now that this was happening, he wondered if the joke was somehow on him.

He strode up to the stage and shook Judy Shane's hand. "Thank you," he said into the microphone. "I don't know why Mark wouldn't want to be here for this. I hope everything is okay."

The audience murmured some more.

"I will be sure to get this trophy to him on Monday, and we will have our own awards ceremony at Ivy Road," he said with a smile. The crowd applauded politely. "But first," Mr. Haverty said quietly to Judy Shane, though the microphone picked it up. "Which Mark Hopper won?"

"Which one?" she asked.

"Yes, there are two."

"There are two?"

"Yes."

The crowd was scratching their heads.

Judy Shane consulted her notes. "Mark Geoffrey Hopper. Geoffrey with a *G*."

"Yes, there are two."

"There are two?"

"Yes."

The press began to snap pictures of Mr. Haverty and Judy Shane, awkward and puzzled.

"Well, you can figure that out with the committee after we finish up here," Judy Shane said with confused smile.

Emily stood up from the front row. "He has brown hair, side-parted. And lots of freckles," she offered.

The principal sighed and shook his head.

Dr. Latchky approached the principal, the politician, and the podium. "Maybe we should just have someone deliver the trophy to the address on his application," Dr. Latchky whispered. Once again, the microphone picked it up.

"I'll take it," said Grace.

"You have his address!" shouted the principal. The audience covered their ears it was so loud. "That ought to get to the bottom of it. I'll take the trophy and be sure he gets it, and I'll take the painting you were talking about."

Dr. Latchky took Mr. Haverty's arm and led him away from the podium. "We seem to have temporarily misplaced the painting," she whispered.

"The painting isn't here?" Mr. Haverty said, loud enough for the microphone to catch it and share it with the crowd.

"There's no painting?" shouted someone.

"And no Mark Hopper?"

"No, there are two Mark Hoppers."

"But neither is here."

"And neither is his painting."

"This is very fishy."

"This is rigged!"

"Give the award to someone real!"

"Yeah! How do we know Mark Hopper even exists?"

"Give it to someone who's here to accept it."

"Yeah, give it to Grace!"

"No, give it to one of the runners-up, at least. Give it to Harrison."

"Only if he shares it with Emily!"

Dr. Latchky tried to quiet everyone down, but it was no use. Mr. Haverty decided officially that trying to sort out the two Marks was not worth the trouble. "You know what," he said. "Just mail the trophy to his home. I don't want to get involved."

Chapter 36

Mark's Dad's News

"Keep your eyes closed, Grandpa!"

"They're closed, they're closed."

"You're peeking!"

"Only because I don't want to walk into a wall. It's a good thing Beth doesn't have her driver's license yet."

"Grandpa!"

"Just kidding, Beth. You're doing a dynamite steering job."

"Almost there," said Mark's mom.

"Just a few more steps," said Mark's dad.

"This way, this way," Mark guided. He ran ahead to make sure his painting was there. He stood and looked at it for a moment. He positioned Grandpa Murray right in front of the painting. Grandpa Murray turned to the side, and Mark laughed and turned him back toward the portrait. "Okay, open up! Happy birthday!"

He did. There he was, face-to-face with the portrait of himself he was supposed to be seeing for the first time. It was perfect. Absolutely perfect, from the chip in one of his teeth to the way the newspaper was folded to the sparse hairs on his head. "You got me a mirror?" he asked. He scratched his head, but the image on the wall didn't. "A mirror that shows you only at your best."

Mark beamed. "It's not a mirror."

Grandpa Murray reached out. He looked at Mark, who nodded. He touched the corner of the canvas. "When did you snap this picture of me?"

Mark laughed. "Come on, Grandpa. I painted it."

"You did?"

"Yes."

"My grandson painted this work of art?"

"I did!" Mark grinned.

"Isn't it beautiful?" asked Mark's mom.

"Well, of course," said Grandpa Murray. He posed. They all laughed.

"Do you like it?" Mark asked.

"I love it. You are the most talented artist in all of the continental forty-eight states."

"Why not Hawaii or Alaska?" asked Beth.

"Well, probably there, too, but we don't want Mark to get cocky."

"I'll take just the forty-eight states," said Mark.

Grandpa Murray scooped Mark up and squeezed him tightly, then gave him a big, wet kiss on the side of the forehead.

220

"Grandpa!" Mark felt his ears turn red, for he saw Jonathan and Jasmina walking down the hallway. They waved and started galloping toward him.

"How did you get it to be displayed here in the library?" Grandpa Murray asked.

Good question, Mark thought.

"There it is!" Jonathan said when he and Jasmina reached the painting.

"Yep, it's here," Mark said, trying to hide his relief.

"Mark is the only sixth grader who had a painting picked to be hung in the library," Jonathan told the Hoppers. "He's like the art-club celebrity. I painted a portrait of Superman, but it wasn't picked."

"Whoa," said Jasmina. "What happened to you? That is so weird—Mark also has a black eye." She stopped herself, then looked at Mark with her eyebrows raised. "Oh, boy. What did he say to you?"

Mark shrugged, motioned toward his parents, and took a few steps down the hall. "It's fine," he said. "I'm okay."

"Speaking of Mark, you know the Mastermind tournament was yesterday? He didn't go to the awards ceremony."

"Really?" Mark's left eye widened, but his right stayed in a half squint.

"I know," Jasmina said. "My little brother and I were going to go to the ceremony with him and his mom and sister. But when we went over to his house, he said he wasn't going to go to it. I figured maybe he did really badly in that teamwork part, or the interview, so he didn't want to go because he wasn't going to win. But he said he thought he did probably win; he just didn't even want the trophy."

"Why not?"

"Beats me. He said he didn't deserve it. I think he really must be lying because he didn't do well, but he didn't sound like it. He was kind of in a down mood, though. Turns out his parents are officially getting divorced."

Jonathan walked up and winced at the sight of Mark's eye. "Ouch," he said. "Does it hurt?"

Mark reached up and touched it. It was no longer puffy, but it still had a black pouch underneath it. "Not that much anymore. It's a little bit sore, but it'll be okay."

Mark's dad and grandpa approached the group. "Do I get to keep this birthday present," Grandpa Murray asked, "or will I have to come to the library every time I want to look at it? I'm not going to have to take up reading, am I?"

"It'll be up until the end of the year, but then I can take it home."

"But you should take up reading anyway, Grandpa," said Beth.

"The end of the year, you said, Mark?" asked Mr. Hopper.

"Yeah. I can take it home in January, I think."

"So it'll move in with me."

"What?" asked Beth, suddenly appearing at her dad's side.

"I said that the painting and I will move in at the same time," Mr. Hopper repeated. "Well, actually, I'll get there about week before it does, at Christmastime."

"You're moving in with us at Christmas?"

"Well, that was the plan," Mr. Hopper said with a shrug. "The house will be officially sold this week, and I start my new job the first week in January."

Beth threw her arms around her father and Mark threw his

arms around her. "I knew it!" Mark shouted. A librarian stuck her head down the hallway and put a finger to her lips, so Mark just hugged him tighter and celebrated in silence.

"Beth," said Mrs. Hopper, "that means you're going to have to move your bug colony from the garage so that Dad can park his car in there."

"It's not a colony, Mom, it's a lab. But I will. I'll do anything to make room for Dad."

"Me too!" said Mark. He would do anything to complete his family, he realized, even something that wasn't really right, if he really thought it had even the slightest chance of working. He wondered how he'd feel if he had risked everything for a plan that ended up failing. He decided he'd feel like he needed a second chance, even if he didn't deserve one.

"What do you think?" Mr. Hopper said. He tousled Mark's hair. "Can Greenburgh handle one more Hopper?"

Mark and Jasmina and Jonathan looked at one another. They laughed.

"I think it can," said Grandpa Murray. He winked at Mark.

Mark thought. "I think so, too."

Chapter 37

The Trouble with Mark Hopper

Jonathan and Jasmina went back to Mark's house to celebrate Grandpa Murray's birthday. Right after Grandpa Murray blew out the candles on his cake, the doorbell rang. It was Mark.

"Hey," said Mark.

"Hey. I came to say I'm sorry for stealing your painting."

"Are you really sorry?"

"Really, really, exponentially sorry."

"Exponentially?"

"Yeah."

"Okay," Mark sighed. "How's your eye?"

"It kind of hurts," Mark admitted. "You punch hard."

"Really? Cool. Thanks. You do, too."

"Thanks."

Mark looked at Mark. He wanted to say, "I'm sorry about

224

your parents," but instead he said, "Jasmina told me you didn't go to the awards ceremony. Is that true?"

"Yeah. If they said Mark Hopper won, it'd be you. How come *you* didn't go?"

Mark shrugged. "What good would that trophy do me? I didn't even enter. It would just get us in trouble."

"It wouldn't do me any good, either. It's just a stupid trophy."

"Yeah." Mark laughed. "It is just a stupid trophy . . . I wonder who won it, though."

"You really might have."

"You think?"

"Duh. You're Mark Hopper. That name means excellence."

Mark laughed. "That's true."

Mark took off his backpack and took out a stack of books and folders. "Here," he said, holding them out to Mark.

"What is this?"

"I photocopied all of my notes and tests. To help you study for the big tests we have before Christmas break. So you can stay in honors classes." He looked down and started running the tip of his foot along the frame of the door. "I can keep helping you, too, but only if you want."

"Thanks." Mark took the stack. "What're these?" he asked, holding up a couple of items from the top of the pile.

"It's what it looks like. A blue ribbon for spelling, and a book about Albert Einstein. To inspire you."

"Thanks."

"Oh, and one more thing." Mark took a folded-up piece of paper from his pocket and handed it to Mark. He stood awkwardly on the porch kicking around a pebble while Mark read it.

Reasons you should consider giving me a second chance (even though I don't really deserve it):

1. I am very sorry for taking your painting and lying to you about it.
2. I want you to stay in honors classes, and I can help you.
3. The tournament is over (and I don't care about winning it anymore anyway), so I have more time to learn how to be a nice person, and you are the best person to teach me.
4. We have the same name, so it'd be confusing if we were enemies.
5. Together we're unstoppable (evidence includes Operation: Bug Dump and Operation: Mastermind).
6. We need to figure out what to do if Mark Hopper really did win and the newspapers come wanting to interview one of us.

Mark's eyes widened. "What will we do if they come wanting to interview us?"

"Well," Mark said. "I thought of two plans. If you want, I can tell the truth. I can tell them that I forced you to go in my place."

"I don't know if they'll believe that."

"No . . . we might still both get in trouble. But I'll be in more trouble."

"What is the other plan?"

Mark puffed out his chest—though not too far—and smiled—though without much scowl. "The other option is just to confuse everybody. And convince them that everything got all mixed up because we have the same name."

Mark's eyes widened. He looked back at number five on the list: *Together we're unstoppable.* He smiled. "Do you want to come in and have some birthday cake? We're having a caveman birthday—no utensils! It's really fun. Jasmina and Jonathan are here."

"Did you tell them what happened?"

Mark shook his head.

"So they don't hate me?"

Mark shook his head again.

Mark wanted to hug Mark. But instead he just said, "Thank you."

"You know," Mark replied, his wide eyes shining, "if you keep saying 'thank you' and I keep getting good grades, people really won't know which Mark Geoffrey Hopper is which."

Mark scratched his head in feigned confusion. Then he grinned. "There are two?"

Elissa Brent Weissman

went to junior high with two Evan Zuckers, and she always felt
bad for the *nice* Evan Zucker, since the other Evan Zucker was
not so nice. She lives in Baltimore, Maryland, where she teaches
writing to adults, college students, and gifted-and-talented children. She is the author of *Standing for Socks.* Visit Elissa on the
web at www.ebweissman.com